"The author portrays a bea⌐ ⌐ ⌐ ts. *The Zella Chronicles* is a tou ⌐ at people encounter in life. A ⌐ ⌐d understand how God is alwa ⌐ ll encourage and build your fa⌐ ⌐ ⌐⌐⌐ ⌐⌐⌐ these inspiring stories. If you are grieving or confused over life's trials, you will find comfort in these pages.... a great addition to any library."

—*Pastor R. M. Lawrence, Sunnyvale, California*

"I can say the story line drew me in right away. The concept of a young girl growing from completing assignments on Earth to hurting souls in need of help and guidance was a compelling and hopeful idea to explore in the world of fiction. Thank you for penning this story, I hope it is widely read!"

—*Wendy Willoughby,*
Christian Music Director and avid reader of fiction

"Such a joy to read a well-written book. . .loved it and look forward to more from you. We all need to know about the protective power of God."

—*Sis Kathryn Koch, pastor's wife*

To Helen,
May God be with you,
Bless and Keep you!
Anita Tosh

THE
ZELLA
Chronicles

A NOVEL

Anita Tosh

Mobile, Alabama

The Zella Chronicles
by Anita Tosh
Copyright ©2016 Anita Tosh

ISBN 978-1-58169-610-3
For Worldwide Distribution
Printed in the U.S.A.
Gazelle Press
P.O. Box 191540 • Mobile, AL 36619
800-367-8203

Contents

Preface

It is wonderful to have a hope that reaches beyond the grave. Jesus proved that there is a happy land of promise over in the great beyond. The Pharisees, like Job, believed that we pass on to life eternal, and Jesus taught us much about this. He let us know that we would have a glorified body like his glorified body. After his resurrection Jesus could appear and disappear, as well as change his appearance. He could rise up from the earth, as well as eat and visit with his disciples.

These are ideas borrowed and used in *The Zella Chronicles*. She will sometimes be seen, other times remain unseen, change her appearance, and also travel from heaven to earth and back again.

We too will one day have a body like this!

When we know Jesus, we truly have a glorious hope!

Prologue

Zella jumped high up in the air and hovered there to have a look around at her special place. A delicious breeze gently lifted her long brown hair as she surveyed the lush and colorful foliage. Purple flowers, her favorite, were abundant, as were many fruit and nut trees. She caught her breath and spun around with joy. It was her very own! Wow!

Her friends, Jacob, Mary, and Elizabeth already had their special places. Mary had escorted Zella to heaven from earth when she first arrived. She also taught her about life in heaven. Zella remembered the fun they had when Mary taught her how to move through the air. It looked so easy when Mary did it. Zella had several false starts, going up in the air and then falling back down. Mary's dark almond-shaped eyes became slits as her big smile filled her face. She tipped her head back and roared with mirth, making her long black hair reach to her knees. Zella joined the laughter. No one could be sad or injured here.

She met Jacob, Elizabeth, and many more in what they called nursery heaven. It was a beautiful place with people and animals of all kinds. New arrivals learned what they needed to know about life here. When they were ready, each one was given their own special place.

Her special place was not too far from Mary's, which made her happy.

Once she had a look around, she would have some friends over to play. She thought of the fun they could have playing tag in the meadow or hide-and-seek in that clump of trees. She knew Jacob would love it. They had played in his special place before and he loved hide-and-seek.

She heard some kittens mewing and her heart went out to them. She landed near and instantly scooped them up to pet and hold.

Rubbing her face against a kitten she exclaimed, "Jesus, you thought of everything! You are so wonderful!"

The light brightened and immediately Jesus was at her side, "Glad you like it, my little princess."

Zella put down the kitten and jumped up to give Jesus a big hug. "I love it so much! Thank you, Jesus!" She breathed in His sweet scent as she gave him a tight squeeze.

"I think there's everything here an six year old could want, but if you think of anything else, just ask."

"I can't think of anything more I could want. But maybe when I get bigger."

"What makes you think you'll be getting bigger?"

The question took her by surprise, "Doesn't everybody?" With a thoughtful look and a tap on her chin she continued, "Back on earth, I had a birthday party when I turned four. Momma said I was getting to be a big girl. Now I'm six. Am I a big girl yet, Jesus?"

He smiled. "You are a big girl, Zella."

"And someday I'll be big like you and Mommy and Daddy."

"Well, that's possible, Zella, but it works differently here in heaven. Remember when you arrived you were part of a group of Elitas and Elitos?"

Zella nodded.

"Those are names for boys and girls who arrive in heaven when they're young, like you. As long as you're in heaven, your age doesn't change." She looked quizzical, and

Jesus continued, "You remain an Elita unless you accept a mission to earth."

"Earth? But why can't I get bigger here?"

Do you remember earth?"

Her face scrunched as she tried to remember. "Only a little," she said.

"Do you remember there's day and night there?"

"Yeah, I had to go to bed when it got dark."

"Have you noticed that it's always day here?"

"Yes! I can play as long as I like and never have to take a nap!"

"I'm glad you like it. But because it's one eternal day, you can't get older while you're in heaven."

Surprise filled her big brown eyes, "I'll never have another birthday party?"

Jesus laughed, "We can work that out if that's what you want."

Zella clapped her hands and twirled around, "Yea! A birthday party!"

"All right my little Zella, if you like, you can have a birthday party after each mission. That seems a fitting way to celebrate."

"What's a mission?"

"A mission is when you go to earth to help someone."

"What can *I* do?" Zella felt secure and happy in heaven, but the thought of going to earth was unsettling. "I'm still pretty small," she said.

"Now, didn't I just say you were a big girl?"

She smiled and nodded. "But, Jesus, Your angels are bigger. Don't they help people?"

"I send my angels with messages from time to time and

3

they help accomplish My will, but you can help me with many important things. And don't worry, you know I am as close as the mention of my name."

"So I'll never get big without going to earth?"

"The things you learn on earth will help you mature. And that's what you need so you can get as big as your mommy and daddy."

Zella looked thoughtful, and Jesus continued, "I think your friends Mary and Jacob have taught you some things to help you get ready for your first mission."

"You mean being invisible? Oh, that was fun!" Zella's eyes sparkled as she recounted, "Now I know how to be invisible and even make myself look different!"

"Good, but I want you to know that not everything you learn will make you smile. There's a lot of sadness on earth."

"I don't think I remember what sadness is."

"I understand. You have seen no sadness here because no sin is allowed here. Sin opens the door for every evil, wicked, sorrowful, and painful thing. If you can help lead someone away from sin, you'll save them from a lot of pain and sorrow."

"You think I can do that?"

"I'll be there with you, and I won't give you anything to do that you can't manage. You trust me, don't you?"

She hugged him. "I sure do!" Zella looked up into his face, "I'll do whatever you want. How do I start?"

"I'll escort you to earth. There's a small boy that needs your help. Do you remember how Mary helped you when you first arrived?"

"Yes," she said as his meaning dawned on her.

"The rest of this mission is a bit more complicated. You'll just have to be there and you'll know what needs to be done." He held out His hand to her. "Shall we?"

Zella felt bigger already as she took his hand.

"Let's go," he said with a smile.

And the two went upward through the air and out of sight and then headed down toward planet earth.

ONE

Harvey
Arkansas 1916

As earth came into view, Jesus gave some instructions to Zella. "First, Little Harvey will need your help. After that, you'll need to help his dad, Big Harvey."

Zella gave him a questioning look and he continued, "People on earth often do not understand my ways. They are quite different from the ways of humans. Sometimes, when things don't turn out the way they expected, people can become bitter and stop trusting me."

"That would be terrible," Zella replied, shaking her head sadly.

They hovered over a tiny house almost hidden beneath trees and vines. A young man was just arriving home from town with a few scant supplies in his wagon. He greeted his young bride and small son with a big hug, encompassing both of them.

Jesus turned to Zella and gently asked her, "Do you think you're ready?"

Zella nodded her head and gave Jesus a tight hug.

"Remember, first, you'll be there to comfort Little Harvey, and then his dad will need your help. We can't let his grief destroy his faith."

"I'll do my best, Jesus." Looking into his eyes, she added, "I love you."

"I know you do; I love you too." He kissed the top of her head and added, "Just call if you need me." They waved to each other as he departed, and then Zella's attention returned to the home below.

Ↄ

"Here's the flour," the young man said, picking up a large sack. Someday we'll have our own mill to grind our own flour, won't we, Birdie?"

"We sure will, Harv. You can do anything you put your mind to." Birdie's green eyes sparkled as she praised her tall, blond husband. He was handsome in a rugged sort of way, with a square chin and deep set eyes. Birdie's red hair glistened in the sunlight as Harvey looked down at her. The sight was so lovely, he thought, *I'd do anything for you.* But he swallowed the words and turned to the wagon. Pulling out the next sack, he continued, "And here's the cornmeal." He lifted it up, stowed it in his other arm, and carried them into the house.

After putting the two sacks down on the table, he dug in his pocket. "Here's the thread you needed and your new needle," he said, proudly handing over the sewing supplies. Harvey winked as he dug in another pocket. "And, guess what? Lowell was at the mill and I got us some popping corn!" He pulled out his handkerchief bulging with the prize.

"Oh!" She clapped her hands and turned toward Little Harvey. "We're going to have popped corn!" Birdie squatted down to her baby's level, which was getting harder to do with his little brother or sister on the way. She asked him, "Now, what do you think about that?"

"Pa corn," he tried to repeat as he clapped his hands and giggled. The towheaded toddler stomped his feet as he ran around in a circle and clapped his hands.

"I think he likes it," Harv smiled and went back out to take care of the mule and wagon. He sang a hymn as he walked, thanking God for his abundant blessings. His calloused hands gently unharnessed Ol' Bob then brushed, fed, and watered him.

The bellows of Bertha, the cow, reminded him it was milking time. As he settled in to the chore, he thought of how pleased he was to be almost finished with the plowing—thirty-five acres done and only five more to go. That last five would have to wait till Monday, though. Tomorrow was Sunday, and no God-fearing man would think to work on Sunday. He carefully carried the full milk pail back to the house, pausing briefly at the backdoor to admire the view from Buckhorn Mountain. He looked up and breathed a heartfelt *Thank you, Jesus,* and went inside.

The three of them enjoyed their dinner of mush with plenty of butter and milk. After cleaning up, Birdie got out a long handled pan and a small metal cup to melt some butter for the popcorn. As they gathered in front of the fire, Harvey poured the kernels into the pan as his little namesake watched. After securing the lid, he held the pan over the fire. Shake, shake. Pause. Shake, shake, shake. Ping! Little Harvey's eyes got big and round at the sound. More pings brought giggles and a smile. Soon the pings came in such a fury that Little Harvey clapped his hands and laughed. "Pa corn! Pa corn!"

When the popping stopped, Harvey pulled the steaming pan out of the fire and carefully removed the lid.

Little Harvey saw the snow-white cloud inside the pan, and danced around and squealed. "Pa corn, pa corn!" he shouted happily. After Harvey poured the treat into a bowl and drizzled it with the melted butter, they sat together enjoying it.

Birdie gave Little Harvey a single popped corn to taste. It disappeared into his mouth with a crunch and a smile. He lifted pudgy hands to ask for more. Since only one or two were dispersed for each bite, he must have found these servings rather skimpy so he wiggled closer and grabbed a handful. He instantly shoved as many as he could into his mouth. Happy with his successful grab, he began to laugh, but his laugh was cut short. As he breathed in, a kernel became lodged in his windpipe. Birdie scooped him up and cleaned out his mouth with her fingers while Harvey pounded his back. The kernel only swelled and became more securely stuck. The boy was turning blue as his loving parents worked on him to no avail.

"Mama, Mama!" Little Harvey squealed.

"She can't hear you, Harvey," said Zella. "They love you, but they have to let you go."

"Mama, Papa! Papa!" Little Harvey tried to grab his parents, but his hands went right through them. He was confused and afraid, but Zella was there, and her touch comforted him. She cradled Little Harvey in her arms while he buried his head in her shoulder. When he had cried himself out, it was time to move on.

"Look, Little Harvey, look at that bright light." Zella pointed to a faraway light in the heavens. Once he looked at the light, the presence of God drew him, and he took her hand. Together they glided up to the light.

Zella introduced Little Harvey to the other children in nursery heaven, close to the throne of God. Often they would sit upon Jesus' lap and always they could feel his love surrounding them.

Once Little Harvey was happily settled, Zella was ready to return to earth for the second part of her mission.

Jesus took her hand, "There's something I want to show you."

Soon they were back over Arkansas, but this time Jesus took Zella to another house. There she saw an elderly black man, Mr. Williams, alone in his small home. He was praying for his grandson, who was sick with scarlet fever.

"This man has faith enough to help Harvey. Do you understand?"

"Maybe."

Jesus showed her the next couple of weeks as if she were flipping pages of a book. Zella saw Birdie shaking with sobs as she prepared her baby for burial. She wrapped the baby quilt around him that she had made to keep him warm. *He'll never be warm again* she thought as she held him close for the last time.

Her husband couldn't watch. He turned to the window but did not see the awesome panorama before him; instead he had visions of his firstborn son with his happy smile and incredible eyes, so like his mother's. He had felt so complete with Little Harvey. Now there was a gigantic void in his heart. The blue, lifeless face haunted him. His mind reviewed that fateful night over and over again. Was there anything he could have done differently to save his young son's life? His feeling of helplessness turned to anger. Looking up to the sky, he silently questioned, *God, why?*

Why did you take my boy? No answer came. His head bowed and shoulders hunched as grief shook his body.

Realizing there was work to be done, he struggled for control. Going to the door, he said, "I'll be getting the preacher."

News traveled fast. The next morning brought neighbors to pay their respects. The first was Mrs. Piper, a neighbor from down the mountain. She clutched her homemade pie in one arm as she knocked on the door. On a better day Harv would have joked and had some friendly conversation with her but not today.

Mrs. Piper saw his blotchy face and could hear Birdie crying. She handed Harv the pie and pushed her way through the doorway calling out, "Birdie!" Walking straight to her friend, she put her arms around her. They rocked back and forth as they sat next to the baby's body and cried together.

Other neighbors came and went, offering condolences and food. Harvey had gone to help dig the grave. By that afternoon the preacher led a small group of mourners to the little cemetery for a graveside service.

The preacher and his wife returned to their home with them to talk and pray with the young couple. Harvey stiffened at the touch of the preacher but allowed him to lay his hand on his shoulder to pray. The other three wept as they prayed. Zella had never seen anyone cry in heaven, and this great sadness was very moving. She wondered what it was like for her own parents when she had first gone to heaven.

Harvey stayed home from church since the day of the burial and hadn't yet returned. It had been three lifeless weeks of going through the motions. The beautiful spring weather was not reflected in his mood. He had no appetite and barely ate at the urging of his wife.

Birdie asked daily if they could pray together.

You go ahead," he glibly responded.

"But, Harv, we always used to pray together. Why won't you pray with me now?"

"I just can't, Birdie. I don't know what I believe anymore. Why would God take our boy?"

Birdie had no answer. She couldn't understand it either, but she knew that prayer helped her through her grief. It was a great comfort. Before she could voice this, Harvey turned and went outside.

ℭℜ

"Do you understand now?" Jesus asked Zella.

"Yes, I see what you want me to do." She thanked him and gave him a hug before he returned heavenward.

Zella could see the bitterness growing in Harvey. It was Saturday, and Harvey would be going to town. Mr. Williams would be on the road just ahead of him on his way to his grandson's funeral.

Zella went to Mr. William's wagon as it rolled along the track. His gray head looked up to the sky and he let the mule plod along, stopping now and then to taste the tall grass. His thoughts were on his family and his God. Unseen by anyone except the mule, Zella lead the animal off the road and over some rocks.

A large bump startled Mr. Williams back to the present. He saw the wagon was completely off the track and stuck. Looking under the wagon he saw a bent axel, and a broken hind wheel. Knowing he could not fix it himself, Mr. Williams climbed back up in his wagon and waited for someone to come by and help him.

It wasn't long before Harvey came rattling along the road and stopped next to the other wagon. "Howdy neighbor, what's the problem?"

"Axle's bent and the wheel's broken. I sho' nuf don't know how this happened. This here is a good mule. He never goes off the road."

"Let me have a look," Harvey offered. It didn't take long for him see the extent of the damage. "Where you headed to?"

"I'm headed over to Darnell." His black face shone in the sun, but it was tears, not sweat, upon his face. "My grandson passed away. Burial's today."

"I'm sorry to hear that, Mr..." Harvey waited for him to give his name.

"Williams."

"I'm Harvey Brace. Come on, I'll get you there. I was going in to Dover, and Darnell's just a stone's throw away."

"That's right nice of you, Mr. Brace. Thank you kindly."

"Just call me Harv—everyone else does," he answered as they climbed up into the wagon.

It was a silent trip for the two mourners as they made their way through the hills. As they neared the little town, Mr. Williams said, "We'll have the service at the school-house. It's bigger than the house and they's lots a family gonna be there."

Harvey thought of the tiny group at his son's graveside. Then his thoughts turned to this man.

"I can stay and give you a ride back if you need it," Harv offered.

"I knowed you's a Christian, now, Harv. I was wonder'n how I was go'n to get home. Ain't no family in Darnell gots a wagon." Then looking at Harv he added, "I'd be honored to have you at the service, Harv."

"Thank you, Mr. Williams," he hesitated, not knowing if he could bear another funeral so soon. But the look on Mr. William's face convinced him, "The honor's all mine." When they arrived, Harv climbed down from the wagon, wondering if he should, or could ask God for strength to make it through this service. He hadn't been talking to him much lately.

Walking into the all black gathering did not feel awkward for long. The questioning look on their faces changed as Mr. Williams' explained, "The good Lawd brought this angel from heaven to get me here on time. My wagon got busted up and along he come. Now, ain't God good?"

Murmurs of agreement went through the crowd even as he wondered how he could call God good with a busted wagon and grandson ready to bury. *Well*, he thought, *he called me an angel, and I know that ain't right.*

This was a different kind of funeral, so different from the few words at the grave for little Harvey with the handful of friends and neighbors who had come to offer comfort. There must be a hundred people here. Where did they all come from? Their singing was different, too, and it touched his soul.

After congregational songs, a young boy got up to sing.

Steal away, steal away, steal away to Jesus!
Steal away, steal away home,
I ain't got long to stay here.
My Lord, He calls me,
He calls me by the thunder;
The trumpet sounds within my soul,
I ain't got long to stay here.

Harv listened, transfixed at the young boy's voice. The
music continued as the boy began a monologue.

I was walking in Savannah, past a church decayed
    and dim,
When there softly, through the window, came a
    plaintive funeral hymn.
And a sympathy awakened, and a wonder quickly grew
Till I found myself environed in a little negro pew

Down in front, a young couple sat in sorrow,
    nearly wild
On the altar was a coffin, in the coffin was a child
Rose a sad old negro preacher, from a little
    wooden desk
With a manner grandly awkward, with a countenance
    grotesque

And he said, "Now don't be weep'n fo' this pretty
    bit o' clay
For the little boy who lived there, he done gone
    and run away.
He was doing very finely, and he 'preciates your love,

But his sure 'nuf Father wants him in that large house
    up above.

Now, He didn't give you that baby, by a hundred
    thousand miles
He just think you need some sunshine, and He lent it
    fo' a while.
And He let you love and keep it, till your hearts was
    bigger grown
And these silver tears you're shedding, why, they're just
    interest on the loan.

So, my po dejected mo'nahs, let your hearts
    with Jesus rest
And don't go criticizing that there one what knows
    the best.
He hath given many blessings, He hath right
    to take away
To the Lord be praise and glory, now and ever,
    let us pray.

A refrain of "Steal Away" ended the piece, and there was not a dry eye in the house. Amidst these strangers, Harvey felt a brotherhood as he released his anger and bitterness and accepted God's will. As Harvey let the tears flow, others thought, *Surely, he was sent from God—look how he mourns with us like it was his own child.*

Zella looked on from above, smiling through tears, and thought, *I feel like my heart is grown bigger too.*

Back in the heavens, Zella played with Little Harvey in the nursery before leading him to her own special place.

"Come on, Harvey, I have something to show you." She took his hand, and they flew through space. Harvey loved Zella's place upon arrival. He squealed with delight at her many kittens. As Zella watched them play together, she mused, *I believe my kittens have grown while I was away too.*

The light brightened, and Jesus was there beside her.

"Well done, my child!" he said as he walked up to her, his arms outstretched. He hugged her and continued, "You have helped a soul return to the path of faith. His grief is lightened and bitterness doesn't stand a chance!"

She looked at him in surprise, "I only did what you said." She smiled as she looked at his face, "God, you are so good! You care about everyone. It was fun to see how you help, and they didn't even know it's you!"

"You are learning," he replied. "I saw how moved you were at the grief humans suffer, and I am pleased you were willing to help someone abandon their grief and bitterness. It was a comfort to the whole family." Stopping to look closely at her he continued, "I do believe you have grown," he smiled. "And you know what that means?"

"What?"

"It's time to call your friends for a birthday party!"

"Yea!" Zella began shouting and jumping up and down. "Mary! Jacob! Harvey! Hey everyone! Come to my birthday party!"

TWO

Eleanor
Arkansas 1928

Zella was playing with Harvey in nursery heaven when she heard Jesus calling her. "Be right there," she answered. Moving swiftly, she was quickly at his throne.

He opened His arms as she arrived and enveloped her in a warm hug. "How's my princess?"

"I'm having so much fun! I was just teaching Harvey how to fly. It's even more fun to teach than to learn!"

They laughed together and Jesus said, "I'm glad you are having fun helping Harvey. Are you ready for another mission to earth?"

"Sure! When do we go?"

"Right now!"

Zella turned toward Harvey, "I'll be right back," she said as she waved at him. Because there was no time here, her trips to earth appeared to take no time at all to those in heaven.

Taking Jesus' hand, Zella looked up expectantly. "Where to this time?"

"Back to Arkansas. You'll be helping Harvey's little sister on this trip."

"Is she coming here too?"

"No, in this mission, you'll be going there."

"Oh, my!"

"Don't worry, I just need you to be a friend and remind her how much I love her."

"I think I can do that. Doesn't she have any friends?"

"She's feeling left out, and we don't want that to turn into bitterness. She's part of a big family, but she's feeling unloved. You see, she's not the favored child, but many people I use are not the favored one, like Leah."

"Leah? Oh, I have met her and she told me her story. It's hard to believe her sister Rachel was more beautiful than her when they were on earth."

"Lots of things change when people cross over to this side."

Hovering once again over the same tiny shack, Jesus completed his instructions as he brought Zella up to date on the family.

※

Looking down on Birdie, she watched as the young mother struggled with both the sorrow of losing her first-born and fear for the new life growing within her. Her faith went through a great test when Little Harvey left her world. Everywhere she turned, she saw visions of the past when a happy little boy filled her world. But Birdie knew her God had not abandoned her. She felt the baby kicking and reminded herself that God was good.

The time she spent on her knees in prayer gave her strength day by day. After a few months she gave birth to a little girl who changed her sadness to joy.

"What shall we name this one, Harv?" Birdie asked as she held the tiny bundle.

"I don't know, Mother. What name do you like?"

Birdie and Harvey had decided that they would only call each other "Mother" and "Father" so that their children would have that for an example. His use of "Mother" reminded her of this. "Well, Father, I kind of like the name Faith." As Zella watched, it was as if pages were turned and time passed with each page. Little Faith stole her parent's hearts. Birdie strapped her to her back like an Indian papoose while she picked cotton in the field with her husband. Little Faith slept most of the time; after she was fed and changed, she slept some more.

The fields produced abundantly, and they worked side by side from sunup to sundown, filling wagonload after wagonload. They made enough from the cotton that year to start building their family home.

In the evenings after dinner, they would marvel at the beauty of their little girl. Soft flaxen hair lightly covered her head. Her eyes became a beautiful sky blue. Her little dimpled hands would grasp at a finger and bring it to her mouth for a taste as she giggled and cooed.

Pages turned and little Eleanor was also added to the family. Her ash-blond hair and hazel eyes belied the quick temper within. Sweet little Faith continued to be the darling of the family.

Less than a year later, Sheena made her appearance. She was small with auburn hair. One day she became croupy, and her terrible cough would turn into "smothering fits" like her father had. Harvey brought in extra wood and stacked it next to the potbelly stove. "You better sleep in here with Sheena tonight to keep her warm. Maybe that will help her get over the croup."

"Okay, Father. You think Faith and Eleanor will be okay by themselves in the bedroom?" Their new home had two bedrooms in addition to a front room and kitchen.

"Sure, they'll be fine."

But somewhere in the night, Eleanor rolled over, taking all the blankets, so Faith crawled out of their bed and cuddled up to Father to keep warm. The blankets were not enough to keep Eleanor warm so she woke cold and alone.

Time passed like the fluttering of pages. These children grew and three more were added to the family: round-faced and dimpled, Charlie seemed to be born with a smile on his face. Later, Clive was added—he was tall, thin and studious. The caboose of this train was Miles Jedidiah or MJ, for short.

Zella watched as Eleanor went up to Faith and Sheena who were playing house under a tree. Faith was the mother and Sheena was the baby.

"Can I play?" she asked with a hopeful smile.

After thinking for a moment, Faith smiled, "Sure, you can be the father, and it's time for you to go to town and get supplies."

Eleanor's smile faded. She knew if she pretended to go to town, they would be gone when she returned. "If you think you're gonna trick me with that again, you've got another think coming!" Eleanor turned and stomped away. "No, thanks, I'll see what the boys are doing."

First she came upon MJ. His diaper smelled pretty ripe. Leading him back into the house, she called, "Mother, Mother, MJ needs changing."

"Thank you for taking care of him, Eleanor. I'm busy making biscuits for supper right now."

"Mother, he's poopy!"

"Yes, dear, just empty his diaper in the outhouse, okay? And get a dry diaper off the line."

"I should have pretended to go to town," she grumbled to herself.

"What was that, Eleanor?"

"Nothing, Mother."

Zella watched another page turn and saw that the three girls were now at school. Sheena is really too young but insisted on going, so she is in the same grade as Eleanor. First grade readers are sent home for the students to practice with. Sheena picked up the book and proudly read for her parents. Page after page was read perfectly and effortlessly.

But when it was Eleanor's turn to read and she looked at the letters, they seemed to be jumbled up and did not make words. She blinked her eyes, trying to focus, but it looked the same. Her reading proceeded slowly and with great effort. When she finished, she looked around the room at their puzzled faces. Humiliated, she burst into tears and ran from the room.

The next day in school there was more humiliation as each child was called upon to read in front of the class. Eleanor had practiced until she memorized the words that went with each picture. This worked fine until the teacher asked her to read something off the blackboard.

Her hands became clammy as she stuttered and tried to sound out the first word. It was a word from the story, but she had no idea which one. Then, with utter mortification, she heard her little sister reading the words loudly and with confidence.

When it was time for recess, the children all buddied up

with a special friend, leaving Eleanor alone. She hung her head and kicked dirt clods as she walked over to the black gum tree. Once up in its branches, she found some chewing resin.

"Hey, look what I found!" she shouted to no one in particular.

A few came over for the resin, giving her a fleeting popularity. As they all went back to their games without her, her insides churned and her lower lip quivered. *Why can't I have a friend?*

∞

Another turn of the page brought them to Sunday school. Zella could see the hunger in Eleanor's heart as the lesson was taught about "a friend that sticketh closer than a brother." One more page is turned and it is the following Sunday.

Placing his hand on her head, Jesus said to Zella, "This is what I want you to look like."

With his touch Zella's hair became shoulder length and curly. Its dark auburn color changed to mousy brown. Her heavenly attire morphed into a faded blue gingham.

Jesus lifted his hand and she looked down at herself. There were scars on the left side of her body that ran along her arms, legs, neck, and up to her chin and lower cheek. "Why does my skin look like this?"

"These are scars from a fire. You'll appear to these children as an orphan who lost her family in a fire. You're staying with your aunt for a couple of days and then going to live with family in another state."

Zella nodded as the Lord continued, "Eleanor is feeling alone and a resentment will grow if we don't remind her that I am her friend and love her very much."

"So I tell her that you love her?"

"Yes and remind her of the many blessings I have showered her with, and that I am always there."

Counting on her fingers, she enumerated, "You love her, you've blessed her, and you're always there for her. Right?"

"You've got it! And, don't forget, I am always with you too." He smiled at her.

"Okay," she said, as they shared a tight hug.

"It's time," the Lord said, looking down at Zella.

She smiled back up into Jesus' face, happy she now knew what "time" was.

Zella had a basic plan of action and just had to have faith for the details. She blew a kiss to Jesus as he returned heavenward, and she found herself in ragged, uncomfortable clothes walking barefoot down a dirt road. The morning sun was already hot, and the mosquitoes were hungry. She slapped at her arms and neck in a vain attempt to keep them away.

Dust soon covered her feet and legs. She could see the schoolhouse as a wagon passed her on the road, full of happy raucous children, laughing and teasing as they went by. One seemed left out, however. Eleanor looked out the back of the wagon, and was the only one to notice the small girl walking alone.

The Brace family entered the small church meeting in the schoolhouse just before she arrived. Zella took a seat toward the back. A few greeted her as the church began the service. Harvey went to the pump organ and Birdie sat with her six children. The congregation sang a couple hymns before having the children exit for Sunday school. Zella slipped out to join the group under a tree behind the building. She loved the lesson and marveled at how people had to be taught about Jesus. To her, it was unthinkable not to know Jesus.

Today's lesson was on the golden rule: Luke 6:31. "And as ye would that men should do to you, do ye also to them likewise."

The class worked on memorizing the scripture. Once all the children had recited it satisfactorily, they were allowed a few minutes of playtime before they would return to the building for the rest of the service. The children paired up and Eleanor was left with Zella. Thinking of the lesson, Eleanor went to say hello to the new girl. It was strange that she was here by herself.

"Where's your family?" Eleanor blurted out.

Zella looked down, "I d-don't have one." Her lower lip quivered slightly and Eleanor's compassion moved her a step closer.

"You poor thing! Whatever happened to your family?" she soothed, placing a hand on her shoulder. "Are you all alone?" Eleanor rattled off question after question without waiting for an answer.

With lips still unsteady, Zella squeaked out, "There was a fire."

Eleanor took her hand on impulse and declared, "You're coming home with me today. Surely your people won't mind—all the kids come over to our house on Sundays. Please say yes."

Zella managed a crooked smile, "I'm sure they won't

mind at all. Thank you very kindly. Uh, by the way, I'm Zella. What's your name?" They laughed together.

"I'm Eleanor. The boy you sat next to is Charlie, my brother." She continued pointing out and naming the other children until it was time to go inside. Eleanor invited Zella to sit with her, and they enjoyed many glances and nods through the sermon.

The ride home was so much fun that they hardly noticed the mosquitoes! It seemed every child at the church was piled into the wagon. The dust came up behind them as they went, mixing with the laughter in the sunshine. Zella helped Eleanor with her few Sunday chores, then they all enjoyed some cornbread and milk with a helping of greens from the garden. Afterward, the children joined in a lively game of tag. The girls ran till they could run no more and went to sit under a tree to catch their breath.

"You're so lucky," Zella said, a dreamy look on her face. "You have all these brothers and sisters, a mother and a father, and all these friends. Wow, God must love you more than I love cornbread." She smiled over at Eleanor who had a thoughtful expression on her face.

Eleanor didn't really know what to say. Looking around she answered, "I never thought of it like that." Then looking at Zella she thought, *She has none of these things, and she is still happy for me that I have them.* Looking around at her home, family, and friends, Eleanor got a lump in her throat. "I wish you could come and live with us." Briefly she thought how great it would be to have someone to play with all the time. That bubble burst as quickly as it had formed.

"I wish I could, but Aunt Marybelle has her own ideas.

I'll only be here a couple of days," she said sadly.

Then Zella got up with a grin and said, "So we better get back in the game while we can. Tag!" Zella jumped up with Eleanor in hot pursuit.

Church that night was wonderful for Eleanor. Just to have a special friend to sit with made it heavenly. Outside after the service, everyone was visiting a little before leaving for home. "Will you be at school tomorrow?" Eleanor wanted to know.

Zella sighed, "No, Aunt Marybelle don't want me to start school here 'cuz she says I'll be leaving soon." Seeing the sadness on Eleanor's face, she continued, "I sure had a great time today, Elly. Thank you so much for being my friend."

"Oh, Zella!" Eleanor wailed as she threw her arms around her, "I wish you didn't have to go!"

"Me too," came the muffled answer as the two cried together. "You're the best friend I ever had, Elly, and I'll never forget you!"

Zella reached down, grabbed a flower, and handed it to Eleanor. "Here's a forget-me-not, Elly. Press it when you get home, and it will always keep, just like our friendship." She picked another one saying, "Here's one for me. I'll do the same, and whenever we see forget-me-nots, we'll remember each other, deal?"

"Deal."

"Elly, I'll always thank Jesus for our friendship." Tears began to make their way down her cheeks, "And, Elly, when I'm missing you and wish I could talk to you, I'll talk to Jesus 'cuz He's always there."

"Me too, Zella!" Elly said through tears. "I wish you

didn't have to go! I'll always remember you."

"You've been such a good friend to me, Elly. Most people just look at my scars and give me pity. But you gave me friendship. Thank you." The two hugged one more time, "I've got to get back before it gets dark, or Aunt Marybelle will tan my hide." She turned and hurried down the same road she had traveled earlier that day, the dust rising up behind her in the evening dim.

"Elly," whispered Eleanor. "She called me Elly." *That sounds so much nicer than Eleanor*, she thought as she looked at the cluster of forget-me-nots in her hand.

When she got home, after her parents helped her press the flowers, she had an important question. "Mother, Father, can I have a nickname?"

"What kind of nickname are you thinking about?" her Father asked. "When Zella was here, she called me Elly. I like it. What do you think?" Her stomach was in knots as she asked. She hadn't realized it, but her hands were in knots too.

Nodding, he said, "That sounds like a right fine name to me. You want us all to call you Elly from now on?"

Elly threw her arms around him so fast he nearly fell over. "Oh, thank you, Father! Thank you!"

"Okay, Elly, I'll only call you "Eleanor" if you make me mad. Then it will be Eleanor Hepsiba!"

Laughing, she answered, "I'll be good, Father, I promise."

The next day Faith and Sheena came running into the house, "Mother, Mother!" they called.

"Shhhh," came the reply, "I just got the baby down for his nap."

Whispering now, the girls continued their complaint, "Mother, Eleanor refuses to speak to us!"

"Eleanor, Eleanor?" she answered, pretending not to know the name. "Oh, you must mean Elly. Just call her by that name and you won't have any problem," she said, smiling at them. "Now shoo before I think of something I need you to do." Her hands motioned them toward the door and off they went.

Eyes big, Faith looked at her sister, "Well, don't that beat all?"

Sheena was about to answer when Elly came up to them carrying an armload of flowers, "Here's one for you, Faith, and one for you too, Sheena." She handed each girl a handful of forget-me-nots and said with a curtsy, "From your new sister, Elly." Then she walked inside to give some to her mother and also place some in her room.

Her sisters followed, finding jars in which to arrange the flowers. Elly walked through the house, smiling at the sight of the flowers in every room. *It's like seeing you every-where I look,* she thought. *I miss you, Zella, but I'm so glad you left me these flowers for a memory.* She thought for a moment, *And somehow I can't think of you without thinking of Jesus.*

On the way to school the next day, the boys ran on ahead, and Faith and Sheena were whispering secrets to each other as they went. Elly was slowing her step and feeling the old sad feeling of being left out when she spotted what she was beginning to call a Zella bush. Her countenance brightened, and she stopped to pick some flowers for her teacher, Miss Zimm. The sun came out at the same time, and Elly had a smile on her face the rest of the way to school.

After school Elly offered to pick the greens for supper after her other chores were done. Mother was busy and thankful for the help. Zella enjoyed being in the garden. A special bush grew at the far side with the now endeared tiny blue flowers. It was like having a friend there to talk to. *"When I am missing you and wish I could talk to you, I will talk to Jesus 'cuz He's always there."* Elly remembered the words, looked up toward heaven then at the bush, and began to talk to Jesus, her very best friend. This happened so often that she really did feel His love everywhere she went.

After dinner Elly offered to help Sheena with her arithmetic homework. Sheena might be great with words, but Elly found that her sister didn't excel with numbers. When her sister tried her patience, all Elly had to do was look at the flowers on the table, take a deep breath, and say, "let's try it again."

It was amazing how many forget-me-not bushes she now noticed. Why, they seemed to be everywhere—along the road to school, on the way to friends' houses, by the church, and in the garden. Elly wondered if Zella knew what a special gift she had given her with that simple flower.

ଓ

Did you see the goodness in those two sisters?" Jesus asked.

"Yes, I could tell they loved their sister and didn't mean to hurt Elly." She brightened, "And now they won't. Elly spends time talking to you whenever she feels lonely or left out."

"You know, Zella, your mission made a world of difference in her life. You taught her to turn to me and to be thankful. That's going to help her many times down the road."

"Down what road?"

"It's a figure of speech." Jesus smiled. "Now, I have something to show you."

The two appeared in Zella's special place and, there between two trees, was a beautiful forget-me-not bush. As she looked around, she noticed the same tiny blue flowers sprinkled throughout the trees and meadow.

Mewing made her turn back to the nearby bush. Three kittens appeared under the edge of its branches. *They're getting bigger*, she realized.

Then looking up at Jesus, she smiled and lifted her arms to him, "Thank you!" she said.

He lifted her off the ground and twirled her around, "We are true forever friends, my little Zella!"

THREE

Cissie
Arkansas 1933

"See you later, Zella," Joseph waved and then sped through the sky toward his own special place. As he left, Zella heard a voice close by.

"Hello, princess."

Zella knew that voice. She turned and ran to Jesus, "I'm so glad you're here!" After a big hug she continued, "I want to show you how big my forget-me-not bush has grown."

They walked together, hand in hand, enjoying the beauty around them and the feeling of being together. When they got to the forget-me-not bush, Jesus exclaimed, "It's as tall as you are now!" Then turning to her He said, "And you are almost as tall as my shoulder."

Zella beamed with delight as she jumped up and down, "I'm growing! I'm growing!"

"Yes, you are! And I have just the thing to help you grow some more."

"Another mission?"

"Yes, there's an old woman who is very dear to me. She's feeling useless and lonely, and I think a visit from you would cheer her up."

"I'm ready!" She offered Him her hand as she asked, "Shall we?"

"We shall." He took her hand and they headed for

Arkansas once again. The two observed for a bit before Zella began her mission.

❦

An old woman sat on the porch of a small home, barely more than a shack, on the edge of the tiny town of Dover. Her tatting shuttle flew back and forth in her gnarled old hands as the delicate lace materialized.

This was one of her favorite things to do. So many of her past favorite activities were no longer possible for her, but she didn't want to dwell on that. Unbidden memories bombarded her of past gardens, long walks, time with friends, and the sweet times she had going to church. *Goodness knows I can hardly keep my own house clean these days.*

She looked down at her swollen feet. *Now, I wasn't supposed to be thinking about those things,* she chided herself. *I can still tat. I can sit here on my front porch, enjoy the weather, and pray for all my old friends—the few that are still alive. There I go again!*

She looked at the pile of tatted doilies she had completed. *I can still make beautiful doilies,* she told herself, *but what am I going to do with so many?* Looking up to the clouds in the blue sky she asked, *Lord, what am I here for? You have a reason for everything. If I wasn't needed, you would have taken me home by now, only I can't see what it is, Lord. All I can do is tat.*

It was just after three o'clock. The school children began rushing by her house. *They act like I'm a witch,* she thought, then caught a glimpse of herself in the window.

Maybe I look like one with my white hair and wrinkled old face. Cissie sighed and went back to her tatting.

ᴄℛ

"This time you will go as yourself but dressed in the clothes for the time and place."

Attired in a blue and yellow plaid dress, Zella asked, "Now, what am I supposed to do?"

"Cissie has worked hard for my Kingdom and prayed for everyone she knows. Unfortunately, they haven't returned the favor. So you, my sweet Zella, will show her the love and friendship she has been missing and also pay a little visit to some of the church members to remind them of a few things."

"Okay, here I go."

ᴄℛ

Cissie felt someone's eyes upon her and looked up. Sure enough, there was a little girl. But this one did not run away. Could she believe her eyes? The child was waving at her.

Cissie lifted her hand in greeting, "Hello," she croaked, surprised that her voice still had that "just woke up" sound in the middle of the afternoon.

A timed "Hi," floated across the small front yard.

Not having had any conversation for some time, Cissie stumbled at trying to think of what to say next. She looked around, "Nice day."

The girl nodded. Evidently she wasn't much of a talker either.

"Whatcha doing?"

Cissie knew it was unreasonable, but she hated that question. "Tatting," was her curt reply.

"That's nice. See you later, bye," she waved and walked on down the street.

Cissie had mixed emotions. It was kind of nice to have someone to talk to as long as the girl didn't ask a lot of stupid questions. It was then she realized that her visitor didn't ask her number one most hated question, "What is tatting?" This always made her feel older than dirt. Didn't anyone know how to tat anymore?

The following day, Cissie was on her porch again, tatting as usual and being annoyed at the school children scurrying by when, to her surprise, that same little girl stopped again in front of her gate.

The girl smiled and waved, "Hi, my name's Zella, what's yours?"

Something warmed in Cissie's heart. She smiled and answered, "Cissie. You want to come on up and see what I'm making?"

Delighted, Zella unlatched the gate in the picket fence and joined Cissie on her porch. Her eyes widened as she looked at the intricate patterns of delicate lace. "This is beautiful! I've never seen anything like it."

"Oh, I've made lots. Take a look at these," Cissie pointed out a stack of doilies. Conversation came easily after that, and before they knew it, the cuckoo clock struck four. Zella jumped and said, "Oh, I should be home by now. I better go. Thanks for showing me your tatting, Cissie. See you tomorrow!"

"See you tomorrow, Zella," she waved. The joy at the

thought of seeing her again was a welcome surprise. *I should bake some cookies*, she thought as she put away her tatting. *Now where did I put that recipe?*

When Zella arrived the following day, there were snickerdoodles waiting for her. Cissie had also dug out an old tatting shuttle and offered to show Zella how to tat. Zella learned the double stitch, and as she practiced, stories of the old days began to pour forth from Cissie. Zella heard about the days when Cissie had been a missionary to the Navajo Indians, but once she began having trouble with her feet, she had to move back to Arkansas to the old family home where she was closer to town. The schoolhouse used for church wasn't far, but even that short walk would make her feet and ankles swell up and hurt so bad that she would never make it home.

That night, Zella paid an unobserved visit to a few members of the church. The first one was reminded how Cissie had cried and prayed with her when her son had died with polio. Then Sister Willoughby was reminded about how Cissie had helped them out when the whole family had come down with chicken pox. She had come over, made chicken soup, stocked the cook stove with wood to keep everyone warm, and cleaned up the whole house. As she prayed that night, she said, "Lord, it's been far too long and I don't remember saying thank you to Sister Cissie." She thought about it a moment longer and continued, "Lord, you have blessed me with an abundant crop in my garden this year. I do believe I will take some over to Sister Cissie tomorrow."

Zella's final stop that night was the pastor's wife. As she was in prayer asking God about a way to help the missionaries, she suddenly thought of having a bazaar to raise money. All the ladies had some special thing they could bring to sell. *Those doilies Sister Cissie used to make would be perfect. I wonder what she would think of helping us out.*

Next, she prayed about where the ladies could meet for a weekday prayer meeting. Her home was so far to the south of everyone else. She really needed someone who lived in town to host it so that it would be central for everyone. Again, Cissie came to mind. *I will pay her a visit*, she decided.

During Zella's next visit to Cissie, she learned the picot stitch and heard about how a sister from the church had stopped by to see her that morning and brought her some vegetables from their garden. It had been a long time since anyone from the church had stopped by, but Sister Willoughby had promised to come over again the next week and bring more garden produce.

As Zella practiced the picot stitch and made her first flower, Cissie shelled peas and talked about how she longed to be useful again in the kingdom of God. "There must be some reason I am still alive. I just wish I knew what it was."

"We can pray about it," Zella replied.

"I've been prayn', child," she answered, wearily.

Zella stopped tatting and placed her index finger on her chin in a thoughtful pose. Eyes looked heavenward for a moment; then she answered, "It must be time to thank the Lord then."

Cissie's mouth dropped open in surprise. "All right, I'll do that."

The next day, when Zella arrived, Cissie had a big smile

on her face. "Guess what?" Cissie's excitement was infectious.

"What? Tell me," Zella urged.

"I guess you were right—what I needed to do was to thank the Lord. It turns out that the ladies need a place to have their weekly prayer meetings, and my house is in just the right spot. I told them I can't get around too good to clean and prepare, but I'll do my best. And do you know what?"

Zella shook her head, "No, what?"

"Two of the sisters will come over the day before to help me get ready! I'm so excited!"

"That's wonderful! I'm so happy for you!" After giving Cissie a hug, her countenance changed, "I have news too," she continued, "my family is moving to Oklahoma. The doctor says the weather here is not good for father, so we are leaving right away."

"I'm so sorry to hear that. I'm going to miss you something fierce," she said, thinking how empty her life had been before she had come. Then she remembered something. "My nephew is moving there too. You might be in the same wagon train. He said there were two other families."

Cissie took both of Zella's hands for a moment and looked in her eyes, "I'll always remember you, Zella."

"Me too," she mumbled over the lump in her throat. She laughed at how that sounded. "I mean, I'm going to miss you too." Zella was trying not to cry as she reached up to give Cissie a hug.

"You sweet thing, Zella," Cissie said as she reached to her stack of doilies and chose one of her favorites. "The ladies at the church are having a bazaar, and I'm going to put my doilies in it to sell for missions, but I want you to have this one." She handed it to Zella as a tear slipped down her check. "I have only known you a couple of days, but it seems like much longer. My whole life has changed since you come by." Cissie took a breath and wondered at just how quickly things had changed. Then, turning to Zella she said, "When will your family be leaving?"

"We're leaving just as soon as we can pack everything up. I won't be able to stop by again before we leave."

Seeing her sad continence, Cissie tried to pick up the mood. "We better have some more tatting lessons before you have to go. I don't want you just going around in circles."

The two sat side by side, heads bent together as Zella learned how to make a chain and how to attach one piece of work to another. Her first doily was taking shape. She would be able to finish it and give it to Cissie for a going away gift.

"Look Cissie, how's this?"

"Well, that's right fine. I can hardly believe it's your first one!"

"I want you to have it, Cissie." Zella glanced over at the stack of doilies and suddenly felt silly giving her a doily. "I know you have plenty, but it's all I have to give you to remember me by."

Cissie caught her breath, "Well, child, are you sure? Don't you think your mom might like it?"

"I want you to have it," she said, holding it out to her.

"Well, all right, if you say so." She took the small doily. It was only about the size of a coaster.

"I've got to go now. Thank you so much for everything." Zella gave her a teary hug and ran down the steps and out of the yard. She turned back briefly and waved, "I love you!" then disappeared down the lane.

As Cissie tried to tat through tears, three young girls watched from the fence. "Hi," one of them called. "Whatcha doing?"

"Tatting."

"Can I see?" asked the biggest girl.

"Would you girls like to come up here?" asked Cissie.

They all nodded.

Happily, Cissie answered, "Well, come on up then." They did, and before Cissie knew what happened, she was deep into teaching three young girls the first lesson of the double stitch.

Again, time went too quickly and soon everyone had to go. The three new friends promised to come back the next day for another tatting lesson.

Before Zella returned to heaven, she stopped by to observe the Brace family packing up their things in a wagon to make the move to Oklahoma. She wished she could appear long enough to say hi to Elly, but that wasn't part of the plan. So she blew on the large forget-me-not bush as Elly was passing by. A breeze shook the bush and made Elly look at the bush and then up to heaven.

"Thank you, Jesus, for reminding me." She picked a small bunch of flowers and put them in her apron pocket. "And thank you, Zella, wherever you are."

Zella smiled. "I will always be part of your family, in my heart."

Zella went to where Elly had put her things. She placed

Aunt Cissie's doily in a small box of her special things. After all, she couldn't take it with her.

ॐ

When Zella arrived back in heaven, Jesus greeted her with, "Well done, princess!"

Zella smiled and gave Him a hug in greeting, "Thank you, Jesus. It was wonderful to see her smile. It transformed her whole face!"

"Loneliness doesn't look good on anyone. If only more people made time to share the love I have given to them, there would be a lot less loneliness. Thanks to you she won't be lonely anymore."

"You are right about that. Her last years will be useful and happy."

FOUR
Elly
Salinas, CA 1943

"See that young man?" Jesus asked as the two of them hovered over a hardware store, watching a young man stocking shelves.

"Yes."

"He's the right one for Elly."

"Okay."

"I know that and you know that, but she doesn't know that. The enemy is about to bring along a temptation that could take her life in a very different direction."

"I have an idea, but I would need Cissie to help me."

Jesus smiled, "I like your idea. Let's get Cissie."

☙

Elly sighed when she looked at her left ring finger. It was bare—no ring, no engagement. *Will Gabe ever ask me?* Perhaps he needed more than the three months that they had been seeing each other. With all the young men going off to war, people would meet and marry within only a week's time. But Gabe would never be shipped out to the war, so there was no rush.

Looking out of the bus window, she saw the hardware store where he worked, then her own reflection. An attractive face, hazel eyes, good skin, well set hair. But this was never enough when she was with her sisters.

Her own mousy brown hair, dulled next to Sheena's long auburn waves. *Why won't my hair grow? Faith's honey-blond hair is past her waist, and mine barely grows to my shoulders.*

Elly began to think over the events that had brought her to California.

She thought of that day in the cotton field when Beau had called to her and made her heart skip. But he only wanted to ask about her sister, Faith.

Then there was Floyd. He was interested in her until he came home to meet the family. One look at Sheena was all it took, and he was head over heels. *I think he would have proposed right then and there if we hadn't all been watching him.*

It was so frustrating watching every other girl in the church get married. *I was so determined to marry the first young man who asked me. What a mistake that was.* She shook her head at the memory. *After just two days he was gone, never to return.* Facing her family after that disaster was one of the hardest things she had ever done. The look of pain in her mother's face was more than she could take. Day after day it reminded her of the shame of her failed marriage.

After talking it over with her parents, a letter was sent to cousin Kathleen. Soon she was installed with the spinster aunt to finish high school. Getting married at seventeen had messed up her last year of high school. Moving in with Kathleen gave her a chance to start over. She proudly finished at the top of her class.

She couldn't continue to impose upon cousin Kathleen, so the live-in nanny/housekeeper job sounded perfect. It might have been if the father of the children had not taken a fancy to her.

To escape his advances, she married her second husband. This charming boyfriend had turned into a bossy old goat in no time at all. He wanted a girl just like his mother, one who meekly catered to her husband's every whim. *I hope I am never like his mother!* she thought defiantly. *She was nothing more than a doormat!*

Then war tore apart everyone's life. Floyd and Sheena left the farm when he got stationed at Fort Ord, California. Beau and Faith were in Texas. Elly herself was working at a doctor's office, but even the doctor she was working for got drafted. That's when the invitation came from Sheena to come and stay with her. Now that Floyd was stationed overseas, she was lonely and homesick.

They had fun for a while, then Beau shipped out and Faith wrote asking Sheena to join her in Texas. Making her apologies as she packed, Sheena seemed to evaporate into thin air. *Now*, Elly thought, *here I am making a new life for myself, again.* She had her rented room, her job, and Gabe. Could he be the right one? When she married again, it would have to last.

Elly got off the bus a block from the restaurant and arrived just in time for the lunch hour rush. She tied her apron around her tiny waist, checked to see that she had her order pad and pencil, and went directly to her first customer, water and menu in hand. She hadn't really noticed the young man much as he entered the restaurant—he was just another soldier.

Placing the water and menu on the table, Elly looked into incredible blue eyes and froze in place. Their eyes locked, sending a zing through her like never before. Breath caught in her throat and she struggled to speak. "I'll give you a couple of minutes to look at the menu," she croaked and cleared her throat, "unless you already know what you want."

His smooth voice was like hot fudge on top of ice cream. "Oh, I know what I want," he said meaningfully as his gaze lingered appreciatively on her curves. "But I better look at the menu for lunch, " he finished with a wink.

Elly hated how quickly her checks flushed and burned as she answered, "I'll give you a couple of minutes then." She turned and carefully walked to the kitchen on rubber legs, ignoring two other customers in her confused state. She had to get herself together. This guy really rattled her.

No sooner did she get to the kitchen than she heard her boss yelling, "What are you thinking? There are two more customers out there! Get moving!"

"Just getting their water," was her feeble attempt to cover herself. After delivering menus and water to the other customers, she headed back to Mr. Blue Eyes to take his order.

"I'll have a meatball sandwich and a cup of coffee," he said, handing her the menu. He spoke with an accent that Elly couldn't place. Here in California, so close to Fort Ord, it seemed like everyone was from some other part of the country.

She wrote down the order, smiled, and said, "Coming right up." As she walked away she chided herself thinking, *That sounded so stupid!* But it was hard to tear her mind away from the image of those broad shoulders straining his army uniform and those incredibly blue eyes. When she brought his order, she had to be extra careful because her hands felt shaky.

As she placed it on the table he crooned, "Thank you, Elly."

She almost spilled his coffee upon hearing her name. "Oh! You're welcome, sir, my pleasure." Again her brain tried to give her directions, *Don't gush!*

"Call me Axel. I'm sure I'll be see'n you again," he winked. "What time do you get off?"

Her cheeks were red again. *This is infuriating!* "Not for hours," she answered, trying hard to remember her boyfriend's name; *Gabe, yeah, that was it.* "Enjoy your sandwich," she said before turning to her next customer. *Be still oh my heart, this can't be right.*

After work that night, Elly walked to the bus stop. The heat of the day was leaving now, and the evening felt delicious. Gabe would be by later, she reminded herself, but thoughts of Axel kept crowding in. As she pondered whether or not it might be all right to see Axel, a young girl, and what looked like her grandmother came to sit with her on the bench.

"Stay close to me, Zella," the grandma instructed.

Elly looked up when she heard the name of her childhood friend. But of course this couldn't be the same Zella she had known. Her Zella would be in her twenties just like she was. This girl looked only about ten, her brown face framed with shiny black curls. *What an adorable girl*, she thought.

"Si, Grandma Cissie," she answered as she sat down.

The grandmother turned to Elly adding quietly, "There's so many young army men in this town, we can't be too careful, if you know what I mean."

Elly smiled, "I don't know, it kind of makes me feel safe with the base so close."

"Oh, I am thankful for our boys in uniform, don't get me wrong. Most of them are wonderful young men. It's just that a few are only out for what they call a good time. Like that one across the street."

She nudged Elly and nodded her head in the direction of a couple walking together. The girl had on very red lipstick and a revealingly tight dress. The soldier walked with one arm around the girl, and with the other he stopped to cradle her face for a kiss, right there in public!

"You be sure to stay away from men like that, Zella," Grandma instructed. "And don't ever let me see you dressed like that!" she added with a shudder.

Zella gave a vigorous nod, "You can count on me, Grandma. I'll never do that."

"Está bien, Lita." She squeezed the girl affectionately and continued, "Now the young man at the hardware store, he was such a gentleman, wasn't he Zella?"

The girl nodded energetically, "Yes, we got mouse traps and roach spray." Grandma's eyes widened and she hurried on, "Yes, but the point is, you could just tell he was an honest man. When I overpaid, he pointed it out quickly and made sure I had the correct change. He even directed me to the bus stop."

Elly couldn't help but join in the conversation at this point. "I know someone who works at the hardware store. Did this man wear a hearing aid?"

Grandma's face lit up, "Come to think of it, he did. Do you know him?"

Elly smiled, "Yes, and you're right, he is a good man."

"Oh, here's our bus, Zella. Nice talking to you. Bye now."

The two of them boarded, the doors hissed shut, and the behemoth lumbered down the street in a fowl smelling plume of exhaust.

Elly waved away the exhaust and stood as she saw her bus coming. As she boarded, the words lingered in her mind, "He is a good man." She pondered them on the way home. That is what she wanted, right? Still, those blue eyes haunted her.

Later that night, Elly and Gabe were enjoying a walk through the town. They stopped while passing the theater to read about the new film, *Casablanca*.

"Humphrey Bogart and Ingrid Bergman," Gabe observed, "Looks like a good one," he said, looking at Elly.

"Yes, it looks exciting, doesn't it?"

With a smile of relief he asked, "I get paid on Friday, how about we go see it together?"

"That sounds great!" Elly looked at the man she was walking with and felt a surge of affection. *Do I love him?* she wondered.

They continued their walk and Gabe bought a newspaper.

"Let's see how the war is going." He unfolded the *Salinas Californian* and looked at the headlines. "Wowy! Look at all of this. Did you bring the map?"

Elly smiled and patted her purse. The two of them walked to a small park and found a place to sit and compare the news with an atlas. Elly thought of her three brothers and wondered where they were. They charted the course of the *USS Yorktown*, looked for Tulagi and wondered what the Coral Sea might look like.

The light was fading, and Elly had a curfew at her women's rooming house, so they grudgingly headed in that direction. When they arrived, Gabe didn't dare kiss Elly in public, so he courteously said good night. But as she turned to go into the building, he took her hand again, saying, "Tomorrow night, Casablanca," as he smiled into her eyes.

"Tomorrow night," she smiled back. "See you then, Gabe." She gave his hand a squeeze before letting go and entering the building.

Up in her room she pondered over the evening. *He must like me a good deal to take me to the movie. He's always so careful with his money.* Then, without warning, those blue eyes returned to her thoughts. She punched her pillow. *He hasn't even asked me out. Why should I give him a second thought?*

Zella hovered overhead as Elly slept. For a moment she tapped her chin in thought. Straightening up, her hand pointed heavenward as her face lit up. She lightly tapped Elly's forehead, smiled, nodded, and vanished into the next day.

A vivid dream perplexed Elly when she awoke the next morning. In it she walked with Gabe on one side and Axel on the other. Her hand reached out to Gabe—he was solid and comforting. But when she reached out to Axel, her hand went right through him like he wasn't there. In fact, he somehow looked like clouds. She didn't have time to ponder over it. Today was washing day and she had to get up and get busy right away.

Looking out of her bedroom window, she noted it was overcast again. "I'm going to wash anyway. It's Friday and I want to look nice for our date," she said to herself.

As she gathered her laundry together, she remembered how the clouds had fooled her when she first moved here, causing her to put off doing laundry because it looked like rain. Eventually someone explained that living close to the ocean caused an overcast that burned off with the heat of the sun. Now she knew that by midmorning it would be sunny and warm, so she washed her things in a basin and hung them outside to dry.

She needed to freshen up before work, but the time was gone. She put her work clothes on and gave her hair a quick brush thinking, *I'll clean up after work before my date.*

She arrived at the bus stop just in time to hop aboard. When she got off the bus, there was Axel. She self-consciously smoothed her skirt and hair when she saw him.

His face lit up when he saw her, "Well, my day just got a whole lot better! Here comes the beautiful Elly!"

She did not feel beautiful, and the attention in front of everyone embarrassed her, but still she was flattered. "Hello Axel. I've got to rush, I'm on my way to work."

"I'll just walk with you then," he said as he fell into step with her, singing and flirting as they walked.

Elly blushed and giggled in spite of herself as she bumped into her boss who was outside the restaurant. "Oh, excuse me, Mr. DeSoto. Are you all right?"

"I would be better if my waitresses would get to work and stop flirting with the clientele," he yelled.

Elly felt like saluting, but she was far too embarrassed at being accused of flirting. Her anger flared and she wanted to give him an earful; but she needed the job, so she forced herself to reply, "I'm getting to work right now, sir," and she went inside.

Turning to Axel, Mr. DeSoto, who looked like a big bear, growled, "Are you a paying customer?" Before Axel could reply, the bear continued, "If not, move along!"

With a charming smile Axel replied, "I'm back for another one of your famous meatball sandwiches," and he slid through the door.

He went straight for the same table he had the day before, but it was occupied. Sitting at one across the aisle, he watched for Elly.

Before she arrived, a new waitress came to give him his menu and water. Her blouse accented the best feature of her full figure. Her cute face and red lips were framed by jet black curls. She appreciated his good looks as much as he did hers.

"I haven't seen you here before, or I would have been back sooner," he said.

Bobby Joe giggled. "Oh, I bet you say that to all the girls."

"Only the pretty ones," he said as he winked.

More giggles. "Oh, go on now. What can I get you, sugar?"

Elly was bringing water and menus to a nearby table

when she glanced up in time to see Axel give Bobby Joe a pinch on her hind side as she walked away. She playfully swatted his hand with the menu before going to put in his order.

Elly felt like a chunk of ice was in her chest. He hadn't made any promise; they had no relationship, so why did she feel so betrayed? At that moment, she looked out the window and saw the clouds quickly evaporating out of the sky and thought of her dream.

∞

At work that day Gabe had something on his mind. When he saw Herb come in for work, he went right to him. "Hey, Herb, I got a favor to ask."

"You need a favor from me? Name it, pal."

"I need rationing stamps for gas. You got any?"

"You know I do. My car's been broken down for weeks. I can't get the part I need. Everything goes to the war."

"I tell you what, you get me the gas stamps, and I'll fix your car. How's that?"

"Now you're talking! I'll bring them tomorrow, Gabe."

"Okay, Herb, and thanks a million."

The next day Gabe proudly put down the twenty cents needed for the two movie tickets, his brown eyes sparkling. He handed one to Elly and motioned to the door. "After you."

Elly smiled and went through the turnstile thinking, *He is a gentleman. That Italian momma of his trained him right.*

They had brought snacks in their pockets, but Gabe bought a drink and popcorn to share. As they settled in, she realized for the first time what broad shoulders Gabe had.

Soon the lights went out and the movie started. It held them spellbound as they munched through the popcorn. Once the popcorn was gone, they delighted to hold hands through the remainder of the movie. And when Elsa said to Rick, "But what about us?" Gabe gave Elly's hand a squeeze.

Afterward, as they walked home, Gabe breathed, "Wow, that was a great movie, huh?"

Elly sighed, "What a noble thing to do, don't you think?"

"It must have killed him to find out she was already married. I think I would go crazy if the one I loved was married to someone else." They were just passing the little park when Gabe stopped and turned to Elly. Borrowing a line from the movie he asked, "What do you say we get married?"

"Oh, Gabe!"

"Soon," he pleaded.

Nodding, Elly reached out to him, "Yes, Gabe. Yes, I'll marry you."

Speaking into her hair as he hugged her tight he whispered, "I couldn't stand it if you ever left me. You're better looking than Ingrid Bergman, and I'm not taking any chances."

That line thoroughly stole her heart.

As they sat together on a bench, Gabe continued, "I have it all figured out. Can you get off work next Friday?"

"I think so."

"Good, I have enough gas stamps to get us to Reno and back. What do you think?"

"We have a lot to do between now and then. One week, oh my!"

"It's the only time I can finagle my hours at work. Are you game?"

This was a whole new side of Gabe she'd never seen. He was so excited and in charge. She nodded and he went on, "There's a little place coming up for rent the day after tomorrow. You know how hard it is to find a place these days. If we don't take it, it could be months before there is anything else."

The moon rose high as they talked and planned. Later, they walked over to what would soon be their new residence. The converted chicken coop was a dream come true. It was going to be their first home as man and wife.

By Friday, Elly had moved her few things into the chicken coop and said good bye to the rooming house. Gabe put her overnight bag into the trunk of the car, smiled, and said, "Here's looking at you, kid." He opened the passenger door for her on his 1935 Ford, then got in smiling on his side, and started it up. "As Time Goes By" played on the radio. *How fitting,* she thought as the clouds overhead faded away. They smiled and sang along as they headed for Reno and their new life together.

ɑ℞

Zella smiled from above as she watched them drive off, then she headed back to heaven. Jesus greeted her with open arms.

"Thank you, Lord, for helping her choose the right way."

"She just needed that little nudge from you and Cissie."

"And you brought along that new waitress at just the right time," Zella giggled. Then she became thoughtful, "I wonder what their lives will be like together."

"You'll see, my princess. I have a feeling Elly is going to need another nudge before too long."

FIVE

Madlyn
San Jose, CA 1951

"Ready for another mission?"

"Yes! You know I am!" Zella said with a smile. "How can I help this time?"

"Well, it's Elly again. She expected her life to be a 'happily ever after' story, but, of course, it's not. No one on earth is without their share of problems."

"Why is that?"

"I think you might already know."

"Is it to bring them closer to you?"

"Yes, sometimes that is the reason."

"But there are other reasons?"

"Yes, many. You know I only want what is best for my children, but often they struggle with my will or refuse it."

"What's happening with Elly?"

"She must learn to accept my will and also to be faithful in her service to the kingdom of God. She has been neglectful to pray or attend worship service. Now she has herself in a nasty mood and is about to make a great mistake. That is, if we don't intervene."

"Why do we help Elly, and not others?"

Jesus smiled down at Zella, "Someone is praying for her."

Jesus let that sink in for a moment then continued,

"There is another girl someone is praying for as well. Her name is Madlyn. I think we can help them both at the same time."

ᥩ

Hovering over a modest one bedroom home in San Jose, California, Zella and Jesus looked on as Elly came to yet another crossroads in her life.

It was a rainy December day. The Christmas decorations around the neighborhood belied her mood on this blustery night. Elly had been thinking over her miserable situation. She and Gabe had been married for years and there were still no children. Every time they went to see his family, Mama Pajaro would ask, "No bambinos?" What could she say? It just hadn't happened.

Then Gabe had lost his job. The owner of the hardware store where Gabe had worked had a son named Jerry who came home from the war. Jerry got his old job back, and Gabe was out of a job. Now that all the boys had come home from the war, jobs were hard to come by, especially for a man who was deaf. He could hear with his hearing aid, but people felt obligated to hire a vet.

Elly longed to adopt, but there was no money for that. She wanted to be allowed to work but didn't want to be the sole support of the household. The last couple of years had been difficult, and Elly was afraid Gabe was running with the wrong kind of friends. They hadn't been to church for a long time now, and she didn't feel like God would hear her prayer. She and Gabe seemed to fight more and more often. Elly took a suitcase out from under her bed. The radio began to play "As Time Goes By." It was their song. She threw a bed pillow at the radio and the muffled song continued from the floor as Elly covered her face and cried.

"Oh my!" breathed Zella.

"We know her leaving Gabe is not the right thing to do. If we can get them back to church, they can get the direction they need."

Zella sighed, "How am I going to do that?"

"Let me show you the other family that needs help—their home is over here," Jesus said as he led the way to a comfortable looking home down the street. Inside the atmosphere was charged and tense. A man and a woman were arguing loudly as their teen daughter huddled in her bedroom. Broken plates decorated the floor. The large man towered over his cowering wife as he picked up another plate and threw it against the wall.

"They haven't been to church for a while either, but there is love in their hearts that will allow me to bind them together again if we move quickly. Madlyn is the key here. Her parents love her, and Elly Pajaro is a close friend as well."

"I've got it now," Zella nodded.

"You better get going then," Jesus answered. "There's not a moment to waste."

With that, he vanished, and Zella went to work.

Whispering into Madlyn's ear, she watched the girl spring up and bolt out of her bedroom window.

That was fast! Zella thought. She followed the girl to be sure she arrived at the right place. The rain was pouring down while the wind whipped it in all directions. By the time Madlyn got to Elly's home, she was soaked through to her skin, and her wet hair was plastered to her head. Shivering from the cold, she knocked on the door, thankful for the small overhang of the porch.

"I'm sorry, Mrs. Pajaro, but can I come in?"

Elly's heart went out to the girl, "Of course, dear, come in and tell me all about it," she said as she opened the screen door.

Madlyn stepped inside, "Um, do you have a towel I could use? I don't want to get your floor all wet."

Elly jumped as if she had just woken up. "Oh, of course, wait right here, I'll get some for you." Elly disappeared and quickly returned with a couple towels and a bathrobe in her arms. "Here, why don't you go into the bathroom and take off those wet clothes so they can dry. You can use my robe while they are drying. Here you go." She ushered her to the bathroom, saving her million questions for later.

Madlyn came out holding the wet towels and clothing. "What should I do with these?" "We'll hang them over the furnace." The large floor furnace had clothes lines above it.

"This heat sure feels good," Madlyn said.

"Yea, that will help warm you up. And I'm heating water for tea. Does that sound good?"

"It sure does. You know how I like mine, with lots of honey," she said with a shaky smile.

That was one of the things Madlyn loved about Mrs.

Pajaro—they often had tea together as friends. Their age difference didn't seem to matter. "Anything hot right now sounds wonderful," she chattered, rubbing her arms to warm herself.

"You'll be warmed up in no time," Elly soothed.

Looking around Madlyn asked, "So, where's Mr. Pajaro?"

"He's been working out of town for a few days. He'll be back tomorrow." The tea kettle began to whistle and the two went into the roomy kitchen. It was the only large room in the tiny house. When they were both sipping contentedly, Elly asked, "Your parents at it again?"

"Yes, I'm sorry to bother you like this. I just had to get out of there." Her straight long hair was dripping on her lap. She reached a hand up to squeeze it.

"This time it's even worse." Her voice broke as she continued, "It sounded like he might hit her." Putting a hand to her face she sobbed quietly. "I was afraid he would come for me next."

Elly got up and hugged the girl, patting her shoulder. "There now, Madlyn." She wished she knew what to say. Her thoughts went to Mrs. Brooks down the street. Should she call the police?

"Mrs. Pajaro, could you pray with me for my parents? Remember how we used to pray for them every Sunday at church?" Elly nodded, feeling guilty. "Things were better then. Can we please pray?"

Feeling a bit embarrassed that she hadn't thought of this herself, she answered, "Sure, honey, let's pray right now." The two of them held hands and bowed their heads. The prayer started softly but soon gained momentum.

They prayed loudly and unreservedly. Suddenly, they both became quiet at the same time. As their prayer resumed, it was a prayer of thanksgiving. Then the phone rang, and Elly answered it.

"Hello." She looked up at Madlyn, "Yes, she's here. Okay, that would be fine. Oh, and you might want to bring her some dry clothes. Yes. You're welcome. Bye, now." She hung up the phone and looked at Madlyn. "They're coming to get you."

"I hope that means the fight is over."

"I'm sure things are better now."

Madlyn looked up. Her innocent wide set blue eyes imploring, "Mrs. Pajaro, can we go to church tomorrow?"

Nodding, she answered, "Let's ask your parents when they get here." The question reminded her of her own negligence in church going.

The knock was loud, startling both of them. They gave a nervous laugh as Elly went to answer the door. Both Mr. and Mrs. Brooks were there.

"Please come in," Elly said as she motioned them inside. On seeing Madlyn, they rushed to her.

"Thank God you are all right," her mother said. "You gave us such a scare!"

Mr. Brooks hugged his daughter next. "I couldn't believe you would go out in weather like this! You could catch pneumonia!"

"I'm all right. But, Mom, Dad, can I please go to church with Mrs. Pajaro tomorrow?" She bowed her head and half mumbled, "You guys scared me tonight and she helped me to pray."

Mr. and Mrs. Brooks gave each other a surprised look. "You were praying right now?" her mother asked.

Madlyn nodded. "Yeah, we've been praying for a while. We stopped just before the phone rang."

Mr. Brooks wiped his forehead with a shaky hand. "I've got to tell you something."

Everyone looked at him as he continued. Motioning to Elly, he said, "I guess you know I lost my temper tonight." Elly nodded and he continued. "Well, it was just one of those stupid little things that started it. Maggie didn't have my supper ready when I got home, and I just blew my stack. We rehashed every mistake we ever made, and I just got hotter and hotter." He looked at his hands and shook his head, "It almost came to blows. But something crazy happened. I lifted my hand up and right then a light came into the room. It was just a light, but it got my attention."

"Mine too," put in Mrs. Brooks.

Then Mr. Brooks continued, "It was like water on the fire. Everything changed. I couldn't remember why I was mad. I looked at my beautiful wife and just hugged her hard. We had a good cry together and began talking about all the good things in our lives. Of course we thought about Madlyn. But when we went to her room, she was gone."

Mrs. Brooks continued, "We were sure hoping she was here. I don't know what I'd have done if we couldn't find her," she said as she pulled a tissue out of her pocket, giving her daughter a loving look and another hug.

Mr. Brooks took a step toward Elly, "So, what church do you go to? After tonight, I think it would be good if we all go."

When Madlyn heard that, she jumped up to give her dad a big hug, "Thank you, Daddy, thank you!"

⊂⊃

Zella was watching the clock. If they didn't get up pretty soon, they would miss church. Finding a neighborhood cat and dog, she orchestrated a very loud fight under Elly's window. The cat tore down the street, escaped the dog, and met up with another cat under the Brooks' window. Perfect.

Pastor White and the rest of the church folks were thrilled to see Elly and the new family at church that Sunday morning. God spoke to each of them in a special way that day. When the altar call was made, they all felt drawn to pray.

When Elly got home, she picked flowers from the yard and placed the bouquet on the kitchen table. She had unpacked her suitcase the night before after Madlyn left. She too had begun to count her blessings: they had a place to live, she had a job at the phone company, and Gabe had a temporary job cutting Christmas trees. He did work hard, and he loved her. And she loved him.

He would be home soon for the rest of the day, then go back tomorrow to cut more trees before Christmas. She decided to make his short time at home as special as she could. Spaghetti sauce had simmered all afternoon, filling their small home with its aroma. Crisp lettuce and home grown tomatoes mixed with olive oil, vinegar, and spices made his favorite salad.

Over dinner Elly told Gabe about the night before and great service at church that morning. "I was hoping we could go to church tonight, if you're not too tired."

"Now if that don't beat all," he said, shaking his head.

"What, Gabe?"

"I was driving home today and I was getting sleepy. You know how you do, I opened the window to get fresh air. Then I was freezing, so I rolled the window back up. The next thing I know, I'm opening my eyes, and the car is just going around a curve as pretty as you please! Boy! That woke me up real good! I didn't get sleepy again all the way home."

"You mean it was like someone else was steering the car?"

"That's exactly what I mean. It gave me the creeps at first, but then I realized it had to be God. So if you want to go to church tonight, I'm game."

The next day Elly got a phone call from her sister, Sheena. She was crying and at first it was hard to understand her.

"I knew I should never have gone! What am I going to tell Floyd? Oh, Sis, you've got to help me."

Finally the story came out. Floyd was stationed in Germany and had been there a couple of months. Sheena was feeling lonely and bored so when a girlfriend invited her to a small party, she went. The men there had put something into their drinks to make them pass out. Both women had been raped, and now Sheena was pregnant. Could she come and stay with her until the baby was born and would she and Gabe want to take the child for their own?

Hope for the adoption she had prayed for sprang up within her just as sympathy for her sister fought for recognition.

"Yes, Sheena, of course, please come to stay and I'm sure Gabe will agree for us to take the child." She really didn't know what Gabe would think, but she started praying as soon as she hung up the phone.

Looking around the small house she wondered, *Where could we put a baby?* With a start she asked herself, *Where can we put Sheena?*

Gabe came home exhausted from his last Christmas tree run. He was surprised to see his sister-in-law visiting when he arrived. Sheena offered to run to the store to get some bread for dinner to give her sister time to talk to Gabe alone.

When they heard the screen door slam, Gabe asked, "She pregnant or something? Is that why she's here?"

Shocked, Elly answered, "Yea, how did you know?"

"I've got seven sisters, remember? I know what a pregnant woman looks like. So whose baby is it? Floyd's in Germany, right?"

Elly related the story, ending with, "It's terrible for her, but you know how much I have been praying for a baby."

"What? Are you kidding me? We don't have money to raise a baby! We are barely keeping food on the table as it is."

Hurt and disappointment covered Elly's face. She knew he was right, but she wanted to make it work.

The next day was Sunday and Christmas Eve. The sermon about the baby no one had room for really spoke to all of them. Gabe spent extra time at the altar praying, and afterward found his wife. Looking at her tear-streaked face he whispered to her, "You tell your sister we'll take the bambino." He sighed, "Maybe it will even make my mother happy," he shrugged, "who knows?"

The next week, Gabe got a lead on a job at the Juicy Fruit plant and at the beginning of January, he started his new job.

They lived on a tight budget, but Floyd sent money to Sheena while she was there, and the women sewed clothes for the baby and found a cradle at the secondhand store.

Luigi was born on June 18th, and Sheena returned to Texas soon thereafter.

All they knew about Luigi's birth father was that he was Italian. When Elly looked at her new son, she couldn't help but think of the perfect miracle God had put together in the midst of her sister's tragedy. Luigi had big brown eyes, like Gabe, and curly blond hair like Elly's family. "God, you are so awesome!" she said as the baby's tiny hand curled around her finger.

◯ℛ

Zella gave Jesus a big hug, "You did it!" she said. "The light in the middle of the Brooks' fight was perfect!"

"Not to mention, you learned how to do some pretty good driving in this mission," Jesus smiled, and they laughed together.

"Jesus, you are so awesome! That message you gave Pastor White, and the anointing you poured out—wow— the host of heaven were watching as you moved on those souls!"

"Thank you for helping get the Pajaros and the Brooks back on the straight and narrow way. We want them all to make it home to be with us here forever!"

SIX

Theodore
California 1953

"There's someone who needs your help," Jesus said to Zella.

"Another mission?" She smiled up into his face.

"Yes, we have a dear one who is headed in the wrong direction. We simply must get him turned around."

"Lead the way," Zella said as she took his hand.

They watched a young man from above, planning out how to help him get turned around and going in the right direction. Then they made a quick trip back to heaven to enlist the help of a couple friends.

ॐ

The clouds of dust danced around Zygi's feet as he walked by the side of the highway. Every step scraped across raw blisters. He never thought he would have to walk this far. People would usually give a guy a ride.

When he was bagging groceries and collecting carts, all he could think about was making it big. He had worked at the grocery store his senior year of high school and through the summer after graduation. Zygi felt like that was long enough. It was time to make his mark in the world.

But after three days and only two short rides, he was

beginning to wonder. Saying goodbye to Maddy had been the hardest part. She played "Say You're Mine, Again" on the juke box at the diner and cried. Perry Como seems to do that to girls. *I promised her I'd be back.* he thought as doubts niggled the back of his mind.

His knapsack had grown annoyingly heavy over the miles as his guitar "calumped" with each step. His sweaty face looked heavenward and complained, "Do we have to have an Indian summer this year?"

He thought back to the orchards he'd passed as he'd walked through the Santa Clara Valley. There was plenty of shade there. He sure wished he had some now. Squinting, he could make out a tree up ahead. How grateful he was for the promise of a little patch of shade! Hearing a car engine, he stuck out his thumb with only a little hope of the car stopping. After all, he was south of Soledad Prison. Who would pick up someone hitchhiking away from a prison? The car went on past. Didn't even slow down.

The shade took a few degrees off the heat. Zygi settled down to rest and play his guitar. Everything ached. Sleeping out under the stars left much to be desired. Maybe singing would lift his mood. He began to strum, "I'm gonna be a star," he sang, "like no one's ever seen. My songs will rise to the top, and I'll drive a big fancy car." Pausing, he scratched his head and said, "I'll have to work on that some more."

Looking up and down the road, he could see the steamy haze rise from the hot pavement. A slight breeze faltered by. His stomach rumbled, turning his attention to food. Rummaging through his knapsack produced nothing to eat, but he did find Maddy's picture.

Zygi's thoughts returned to his girl back home. Her parents didn't seem to like him much, so he and Maddy had to sneak around to see each other. It was all on account of that church she went to. Who ever heard of a church where you can't date people who don't go to the same church? They just had too many rules. People had a right to do what they wanted.

He picked up a rock and threw it across the road, "Stupid church! God, if it wasn't for you and that church, Maddy would be with me right now." He thought back over the few intimate times they had stolen whenever they could be together. "I wish you were here, Maddy," he threw another rock, "I'll show 'em," he said to the emptiness. "When I'm famous then they'll see." A noise up the road alerted him, and he stood and put out his thumb. He tried to forget his pathetic ride history and be hopeful. His first ride took him from San Martin to Gilroy, and yesterday a truck took him from Gonzales to Soledad. He figured people were more comfortable taking a person toward the prison. He wished he could find someone going all the way to L.A. Now he watched an ancient Ford approach that looked so old that it should have a crank on the front. No matter, it was slowing down—yahoo!

As it stopped, Zygi approached the window, "Thanks so much for stopping!" Zygi greeted the old couple.

"No problem. We're going to King City, how about you?"

"I'm headed to L.A., but King City will do."

"Hop in the back, young man. Name's Harvey, this here's Zella."

"Pleased to meet you, Theodore Zygmunt's the name, but my friends call me Zygi."

"Zygi it is then," Harvey smiled as he pulled back onto highway 101. "Where y'all from?"

"San Jose—been on the road three days now. Mind if I roll down my window?"

"Help yourself."

"Thanks, where you guys from?"

Zella and Harvey glanced at each other before Harvey answered, "We're on our way to the greyhound station. We have a friend coming up from Los Angeles." Changing the subject, Harvey added, "You know how to play that thing?"

A smile slid across Zygi's face, "I sure do. Would you like to hear a song?"

"Do you know 'In the Sweet By and By'?"

Zygi's smile slipped a bit. He felt more like playing "That Lucky Old Sun," but answered, "I may have heard it. How does it go?"

"Key of G, for Jesus," he laughed at his own joke and began to sing. Zella joined in and soon Zygi began to strum along.

There's a land that is fairer than day.
And by faith we can see it afar;
For the Father waits over the way
To prepare us a dwelling place there.

In the sweet by and by
We shall meet on that beautiful shore
In the sweet by and by
We shall meet on that beautiful shore.

It was an easy song and Zygi soon found that singing it made him feel happy. They went on to sing "I'll Fly Away" and "Are You Washed in the Blood?" They were all upbeat lively songs, making the clouds disappear for a time. He had heard songs like these when he visited Maddy's church.

"Here's one you're sure to know," Harvey said, smiling. His rich voice filled the car as he began to sing "Amazing Grace." Zella joined in until her voice cracked and a tear rolled down her face. She looked out the window as the two men finished up the hymn. When they finished Harvey reached over and patted Zella's hand, "It'll be all right now, don't you worry, Zella. God's got it all in control."

Embarrassed by the scene in the front seat, Zygi awkwardly stammered out, "Is everything all right?"

Zella looked up, "I'm sorry, Zygi. That song just reminds me of Elouise. She ran off with her boyfriend years ago, thinking they would be movie stars, I guess. But along come little Shirley and both her parents are still working odd jobs in the day and singing at night clubs at night. That's no kind of life for that poor little girl." Zella sniffed again, wiped her nose and put the hanky up her sleeve before she continued, "Anyway, things got so bad, they finally decided to come home. God does answer prayer." Glancing back at Zygi, she explained, "Elouise used to sing that song at church. She has such a beautiful voice."

"You'll hear her sing for Jesus again, Zella. God is bringing her home."

Zella nodded, "Let's sing, 'What a Day That Will Be.'" Harvey began the song,

There is coming a day when no heartache shall come,
No more clouds in the sky, no more tears
    to dim the eye.

Soon Zella joined in and Zygi began to strum,

All is peace forevermore
    on that happy golden shore.
What a day, glorious day that will be.

They were turning onto Broadway in King City and went on singing all the way to the bus station. When they pulled up they were just finishing up the chorus for the second time. Harvey parked and looked up in surprise, "Oh, I should have let you off back at the highway, shouldn't I?"

"That's okay. I need to see about getting something to eat."

They got out of the car and Zella pointed as she spoke, "There's a little store by the bus station."

"I think that is the bus station, Zella," Harvey laughed. "Come on, let's see if that's their bus."

Back home, Maddy was acting strange. She was not her normal happy self. Mrs. Brooks worried about her daughter. She was somewhat relieved when she heard Zygi had left town. He didn't seem to want anything to do with God, and she remembered how bad things were in her own marriage before they started going to church. She didn't want that for Madlyn.

Now that her daughter had graduated from high school, it was time to find a Christian husband. That's what she prayed for, but maybe she hadn't been as diligent as she should have been in that prayer. Why had God allowed Zygi to come along and steal her heart?

Zygi counted his money—$2.35. It had taken a long time for him to save it up, and he wasn't sure if it was enough to get him to Los Angeles. His stomach rumbled loudly again. He pocketed his money and headed for the store.

From somewhere he heard strands of "Forever and Ever." Outside there was a phone booth. On impulse, he went in the booth and called Maddy. Her mother answered and hesitated before saying, "Just a minute, Zygi." The phone half covered he heard her calling, "Madlyn! Madlyn, I thought you told me he left town."

"He did, Mom. I'm surprised he's calling," she said, excitement and joy dancing in her eyes. She took the phone, "Zygi, is that you?"

"Of course it's me," his voice softened, "I was just thinking about you, I miss you, Maddy." Maddy pulled on the long phone cord and stepped out the back door. "I miss you too, Zyg. Where are you?"

"I'm in King City," he said, feeling a million miles away.

"Never heard of it, is it far?"

"I passed Gilroy yesterday and Salinas this morning—it sure feels like a long way. I've only gotten a couple of rides." Zygi continued with a litany of his trip. When he came up for air, Maddy spoke up, "Wow, you've had quite a time. You really sang hymns on the way into town?"

"Yeah, this old couple are really something. Great voices, I tell you…"

"Zygi, I need to tell you something."

The operator broke in, "Please deposit another dime to continue your call."

Zygi dug into his pocket and found a dime. "Thank you, click, click."

"Are you there?" he asked eagerly.

"I'm pregnant, Zygi." There was no immediate reply. "I just thought you should know; I mean, it's your baby too."

"I, a , wa, wow. I don't know what to say."

Maddy began to softly cry, "I've got my job at the grocery store so I can save up for the baby I guess."

"Maddy, I feel awful. I can't believe this. Listen, I'm coming home. Wow, I'm going to be a, a father."

"I don't want to kill your chance to make it big, Zygi."

Thinking of the Elouise story he shuddered, "Don't worry, baby, we're going to be a family, I promise. I'll be home by tomorrow and we'll make plans, okay?"

"You don't have to do this, you know."

"Are you kidding? I wouldn't leave you to face all this on your own. Besides, I don't think I could stand another day without you. I love you. You know that, don't you?"

"I love you so much, Zygi."

"I love you more."

Maddy laughed through her tears, and the operator broke in again, "Please deposit ten cents."

"See you soon, bye."

"Bye." Click.

Going inside, Zygi checked the price for a ticket to San Jose. It was $2.05, exactly what he had in his pocket. Deciding he could do without eating another day, he put the money on the counter and bought his ticket.

"The north bound bus is loading right now," the man said.

Zygi grabbed his knapsack and guitar and headed for

the bus. He passed Harvey and Zella on the way. "Thanks again for the ride." Zygi stopped to quickly say, "Looks like you dropped me at the right place after all, Harvey. I'm headin' for home."

"Is everything okay?" Harvey asked.

"Oh, yeah. Something just came up back home."

He started for the bus, but Zella stopped him, "Hold on a minute," she grabbed something out of her bag and handed it to him. "You might need this." She handed a small bag to him.

"Thanks, and good luck to you and your friend. Bye now." He waved and turned to board the bus.

"Good-bye, Zygi, and God bless!"

He stepped up into the bus and found a seat. He turned to the window expecting to see a young couple with a child with his new friends, but they were nowhere to be seen. Zygi opened the bag Zella gave him and found two pieces of fried chicken, and a biscuit wrapped in a napkin.

"Thank God," he breathed before he realized what he was saying. He dug into the food, enjoying every greasy bite.

The old woman next to him was even more ancient than Harvey and Zella had been. She smiled and said, "I like to see a young man with a good appetite."

Good appetite nothing, I'm starved! he thought, but replied, "I've always got one of those." He smiled, wiped his hand, and put it out to shake as he introduced himself, "I'm Zygi."

"Pleased to meet you, I'm Cissie," she answered.

They shook hands and chitchatted a bit, one eating and the other tatting doilies. When Zygi was done eating, he cleaned up and settled back into his seat. Soon he was fast asleep.

Once home, things happened quickly. First they had to talk to Maddy's parents— no easy task. Zygi got his job back at the grocery store, and they made a trip to Reno to officially become man and wife. They lived at Maddy's house for about a month while they saved up money for a place of their own.

They found a little one bedroom apartment and were surprised at the response of Maddy's church. They worried everyone there would judge them and hate them, but to their great surprise, everyone pitched in with things for their first apartment. A sofa came from the Pajaro's, and a table and chairs from the Mitchells. One of the men offered Zygi a job. Brother Timothy was a plumber and would train Zygi. Wow, it was too much.

Zygi felt he had to go to the church to thank everyone. At the beginning of the service they started singing "In the Sweet By and By," and unbidden tears began to roll down Zygi's face. Brothers gathered around and prayed with Zygi until he was speaking in a heavenly language. Sister Brooks could be seen dancing and crying for joy as her son-in-law was born again in answer to her prayer.

He was baptized that very night in Jesus' name, completing the new birth of water and Spirit he had heard about. What an awesome feeling! Why had he waited so long?

In the heavens above, angels rejoiced while Zella, Harvey and Cissie danced in celebration up above.

"Glory to Jesus! Hallelujah!" Rang through the heavens as the angels celebrated with them.

Eventually things quieted down and Jesus enjoyed having a chat with Zella and friends.

"The church was so good to Zygi and Maddy. I think that is what made all the difference," Zella said with a thoughtful look.

"I believe you are right," Cissie added. "Just getting a person to church does not guarantee they will turn their lives over to the Lord. But he just couldn't get away from the love of God they showed him!"

"I am so happy when my children love each other like they should," Jesus said. "You never know what miracles will follow!" he said with a smile.

SEVEN
Tilly
San Jose, CA 1969

"Hello my sweet Zella, what can I do for you?"
"Hello, Jesus, I was just wondering, is there anyone that might need my help?"

"I'm glad you asked. There's a young girl who is struggling with shyness. She just doesn"t know how much she has to give."

"I never thought of shyness as a problem."

"My dear, even Abraham Lincoln and Roy Rogers were shy. If they hadn't conquered their shyness, the world would have been a very different place."

"I see," she said, nodding her head. "If you think I can help, I would like to try."

"Come with me," the Lord said as he held out his hand.

Zella knew the way to earth now, but she loved holding Jesus' hand anyway. They zeroed in on the planet, California came into view, and then James Lick High School.

"This is Tilly," Jesus said, "And the girl at the table is Debbie. Both are shy for different reasons. If you help Tilly, Debbie will benefit as well."

God gave Zella the knowledge she would need about each of their situations. Then, with a hug and a nod, Jesus vanished heavenward. Zella hovered over the teenaged girl.

She watched as the girl struggled with herself.

Tilly was standing near to Debbie, a girl whom she had seen in her math class. It was brunch and the halls were crowded. Debbie sat at a table, her face covered with one hand, her back to the crowd; to Tilly, it looked like she was crying. *Should I try to comfort her, or does she want to be left alone?*

Zella materialized into the crowd as another teenager and bumped into Tilly, giving her a good push in the right direction.

"Oh, excuse me!" Zella said. "I can be so clumsy, are you okay?"

"I'm fine," Tilly nodded, "don't worry about it, really, how about you?"

"Me? I'm fine, just need to watch where I'm going, ha, ha. Well, see you around." Zella turned and melted into the crowd.

Tilly was now standing right next to Debbie and had bumped her slightly. She took a deep breath, steeled herself, and reached out to the other girl, placing her hand on her shoulder. She had a sudden feeling of panic. *What was her name? Oh, yeah, Debbie, that was it, Debbie Griffin.* Tentatively she asked, "Debbie, it's Tilly, are you all right? Is there anything I can do?"

Debbie turned slightly and Tilly could see one red swollen eye and tear tracks down her check. "Why do you want to help?"

This surprised Tilly, and she said the first thing that came to her mind, "Why wouldn't I want to help?" Debbie just shook her head.

Zella, invisible again, was doing her best to keep the

conversation going by telling Tilly what to say. Tilly continued, pulling together a boldness she seldom expressed, "I don't know what the problem is, but I can pray for you, if you like."

Debbie pulled out a tissue, blew her nose, and surprisingly said, "Yes," with obvious relief. She looked up at Tilly, "I would like that."

Tilly sat on the bench facing Debbie and covered the girl's hands with her own. Bowing her head and closing her eyes she prayed, "Dear Jesus, you love every one of us and you know what we are going through. You have the power to do anything and we are asking you to touch Debbie right now; give her comfort, strength, and direction. Bless her and her family; show them the way through their troubles and meet their every need, in Jesus' name. Amen." Not knowing what the problem was, she had tried to cover all the bases.

They looked up at each other. Debbie now looked calm, and a little surprised. She rubbed her arms as if she were cold and said, "That was nice. Thank you, I do feel better now." She managed a weak smile.

The bell rang and they headed for class. Later that morning, Tilly and Debbie were in Math class. Tilly's eyes glazed over as she looked at the mess of numbers on the chalkboard. *None of this makes sense. I wish the bell would ring so I could eat—I'm so hungry today.* When class was over, Tilly made her way over to Debbie.

"Hey, Debbie, do you really understand this stuff?"

Debbie laughed, "Are you kidding? This is so easy, I love it!"

"I wish I had your brain in math," Tilly answered. "Say,

Debbie, you want to eat lunch with me and Lettie?" As Debbie thought about it, Tilly added, "We usually eat over by the Science wing. It's nice and quiet there."

A shy smile came to her face, "That sounds good. Thanks. Um, I need to go to my locker first, how about you?"

The three girls sat on the strip of grass between the buildings and got to know each other. They realized that all three walked home the same way and so decided to meet by Lettie's locker and walk together.

Autumn leaves swirled around them on the way home as Tilly and Lettie heard a story they could hardly believe.

"Do your parents ever beat you?" Debbie asked, with her head down.

"Well, I've gotten spanked but not for a few years," Lettie answered. "If my parents are mad at me, they just give me more work to do, like scrubbing the toilet for a week." She tried to laugh, but it did not lighten the mood.

"Yea, I got spanked when I was younger too," Tilly said, "Is that what you mean, Debbie?"

"No. That's not what I mean. My dad comes home drunk, lines up all five of us kids, and beats us one at a time." Her tears strangled the next words, "He is sure we have done something during the day to deserve it." Her hand wiped an errant tear from her face.

"That reminds me of my mom," Tilly remarked. The other girls looked at her in surprise and she realized what they were thinking. "No, she doesn't beat me, but she has told me about when she was growing up. Before her dad got in church he could be really scary."

"Really? What did she do?"

"She told me about one night when she was so scared, she climbed out her bedroom window and went to a friend's house."

Lettie was surprised, "You never told me about that!"

"Well, you would never know now that Grandpa was ever like that."

"What made him change?" Debbie wanted to know.

"God did. It was when they started going to church."

The hope in her eyes flickered and died. "I doubt my dad would ever do that."

"You know, my mom always says prayer changes things."

Zella whispered something in Tilly's ear, and she felt that boldness come over her again.

She stopped to face the other girls, "I've got an idea." Once she began, the words rushed out in her excitement, "The Bible says that if two people pray for the same thing, God will do it. And we have three people! Let's pray every day for God to do a miracle in your family." She held out her hands to her friends, "Starting now." They held hands in a small circle. Bowing their heads, Tilly gave the others a quick instruction before she began to pray. "We all pray out loud at the same time at my church, is that okay with you guys?" The three of them nodded and prayed earnestly there on the shoulder of the road.

This was new for Lettie, someone who always prayed quietly, and Debbie, who had never been to church.

When they finished their short heartfelt prayer, Tilly encouraged them, "God hears our prayers and he will do something."

"Thanks so much." Debbie pointed across the street,

"That's my house over there. I've got to hurry so I won't be late."

"Just a minute," Tilly dug in her purse for a pen and paper and began to write, "Here's my address," she scribbled quickly and smiled, "if you ever have to climb out the window." Pointing she added, "It's just one block down and one block over."

"Thanks, see you tomorrow," She turned and ran across the street and into her house.

The next day at school, Tilly and Lettie were anxious to know how things went. One look was all it took. Debbie's sunglasses could not hide the bruises on her face. Since it was an overcast day, the sunglasses looked really out of place.

"Why didn't you come to my house?" Tilly asked as she reached out to her new friend.

"I don't know where you live and I was afraid to look for it in the dark." Debbie continued, "Anyway, he surprised us by seeming okay when he first got home. But then my little sister set the table wrong and gave him a small fork, so he went berserk."

"He got the wrong fork?" Lettie looked astounded.

"Yeah, any little thing can set him off."

Tilly had an idea. "Do you think we could ask your mom if you can come over to my house to do your homework? You're a lot better at this stuff than I am, and then you will know where I live." She smiled, hoping her idea would work.

"I don't know. I have so much to do when I get home. Mom doesn't usually let me go anywhere." The smiles faded away. "But I guess we could try asking."

Smiles back in place, the girls planned the best way to approach Debbie's mom and ask.

That afternoon the three girls entered Debbie's home together after school.

"Mom," Debbie called as they entered.

"I'm in the kitchen."

"Mom, I want you to meet someone." That brought her out quickly. From the doorway she could see the girls. Relief was evident on her face. "Mom, this is Tilly and Lettie from school." A trace of suspicion crept back into Mrs. Griffin's face as she greeted the girls.

"Pleased to meet you, but I want to let you know right off the bat that Debbie doesn't have time for anything. She's got things to do."

"Yes, we know, that's why we came to help. If it's okay with you, and if there's enough time afterwards, I could really use some help with my homework. Debbie is great at math, and I was hoping you'd let her come over for just a little while."

"We'd get everything done first," Debbie reiterated with a pleading look while the others nodded their heads vigorously.

Mrs. Griffin eyed them for a moment, "Well, I guess we could give it a try," she said slowly. The three cheered. "You'd best save that till I see everything is done. There's a pile of dishes in the sink, now get cracking!"

Three cleaning tornadoes churned through the house. Within a half hour, everything was sparkling clean, and they had Mrs. Griffin's okay to head out the door. They fairly flew down the street. Lettie called home from Tilly's and they settled down to math homework.

"No, when you add fractions, you just add the top numbers, the numerators, it's when you multiply that you flip them," Debbie gently instructed.

"Why can't it just be the same every time? This is so confusing. I'm sure glad you could help me, I would never get this." Tilly paused to look at the next equation. "So here's 2/3 +2/3, so that would be 4/3, right?"

Tilly's younger sister, Anna, came up and answered, "No, that's an improper fraction, you have to reduce it."

"Is that true?" Tilly looked at Debbie.

"She's right."

"Arrgh! Even my little sister knows this better than I do!" They laughed and finished their assignments. "Finally!" Tilly gave Debbie a hug, "Thank you so much. And, look, we have a half hour before time to walk you home. Let's clean up and go in my room for a while."

As they settled in, Lettie asked the others, "So, who do you think is the cutest guy in school?"

"That's easy for me," answered Tilly, "Gigi Pajaro is the only one for me."

"Is he your boyfriend?"

"I wish. No, I've known him all my life, but he's never shown any interest in me in that way."

"I know what you mean," said Lettie. "There's a guy at church that I've known ever since we were in catechism class; now he's the cutest guy in our teen group and all the girls are crazy about him." She sighed, "But I'd be shocked if Reggie ever looked at me." Then she turned to Debbie, "How about you?"

Debbie's face colored, "My parents would kill me if I had a boyfriend."

Tilly smiled, and asked, "Yeah, but who do you like?"

With a timid smile she said, "Promise not to tell?"

Both girls nodded vigorously, "Yes!"

"Of course!"

"Well, you know that guy you sit next to in math class?"

"David?"

Debbie answered with a nod and a sigh.

Chitchat and laughter filled the remainder of their time before the three walked together to Debbie's.

"Can we do this again tomorrow? This was fun!" said Tilly.

"We'll see how it goes," answered Debbie. "Thanks for inviting me. I had so much fun. I hope they let me come over again."

"And don't worry about the housework," said Lettie. "It's always more fun to clean someone else's house."

This became a habit—the girls prayed together, did housework and homework, and if they had time, enjoyed some girl talk. One day as they walked home Tilly asked, "How's it going with your dad, Debbie?"

"I was going to ask if we should stop praying for him. It seems to make him worse."

"Mom always says it's getting the devil riled up. That means our prayers are working."

Debbie looked surprised, "How bad will it get? I think he broke my little sister's arm last night." She paused and added, "and every plate in the house."

"Wow!"

"Yea, he was really mad. He couldn't find his newspaper and blamed my sister. By the time we found it by the bushes, dinner was cold and that was the end of the plates."

"We need to pray harder. Hey, do you think you can come to church with me? We have great prayer meetings before every service."

Her two friends could not imagine anything great about a prayer meeting. Lettie answered, "My family already has a church we go to every Sunday. I don't think they would let me go to another church."

"I think Dad would come unglued if I asked him if I could go to church."

Zella was listening and reminded Tilly about Friday night church.

"I know! If you guys can get permission to come to my house to spend the night on Friday, then you could come to church Friday night!"

"I can ask," said Lettie, then turned to Debbie, "How about you?"

"None of us has ever spent the night anywhere. I don't know." She shrugged. "I'll give it a try."

That night Tilly talked to her mom about the plan. "Debbie is asking her parents tonight if she can spend the night tomorrow night so she can go to church. I want to fast dinner, is that okay?"

After thinking for a moment, Mrs. Brooks answered, "That's a good idea. I'll fast with you." Later, at family devotions, the whole family had special prayer for the Griffin family.

The next day at school, Lettie told Tilly she had permission from her parents, and the two waited for Debbie. Their hearts fell when they saw her. The stringy hair could not hide the fresh bruise on her face. She was limping, but when she saw her friends, she smiled and went to them.

"Good news!"

"You look like that, and it's good news?" Lettie asked.

"I'd hate to see bad news," Tilly added.

"Wait, let me tell you what happened. He did blow up last night when I asked about spending the night. He thought I was going to go out with boys—that's why I look like this."

"And there's good news?"

Debbie smiled and winced a little. "Yea, this morning, Mom told Dad about how you guys have been coming over every day to help around the house. I heard my dad say, 'You gotta be kidding.' He's usually better in the morning, but this was a miracle. He came to me and apologized! He's never done that! And then he really surprised me by saying I could go!"

The girls cheered and Debbie said, "I'd jump up and down, but it hurts."

"Oh, you poor thing!"

"It's all right, I got a yes! God did it!"

When they got to Tilly's house that afternoon, time flew by as they tried on Tilly's clothes, did their hair, and helped Tilly's littlest sisters, Anna and Zella, with their hair. The family was headed to the station wagon, when little Zella's dress caught on a rose bush and ripped. She ran back in and changed as fast as she could, but when the family arrived at church, prayer was already in full swing.

Zella watched from up above and thought, *Wow, there are other people with my name.*

Tilly had tried to prepare her friends, but nothing could prepare them for what was to come. As they entered the ladies' prayer room, the noise level was shocking. Women were kneeling, walking, and sitting, and all of them were praying loudly. Some were wailing, others seemed to be babbling and crying. The lights were low, and it took a moment for their eyes to adjust. Tilly had to speak directly into their ears, one at a time, for them to hear.

"How do you want to pray?"

"Can we just pray like we always do?"

Tilly nodded and the three held hands and began to pray. But rather than bowing her head like she usually did, Tilly lifted her head and prayed loudly, "Wonderful Jesus, you are so awesome! Thank you for making this night possible and thank you for working miracles in Debbie's life and family!"

Prayer continued for another twenty minutes; then, as music was heard in the sanctuary, people filtered out of the prayer room and found their seats in the sanctuary.

The music surprised the girls too. It was loud and contemporary. They liked it and clapped their hands with the others. But they were amazed at the exuberance with which people worshiped in this church. Their jaws dropped as men, women, and children ran the aisles, jumped, twirled, and danced. Tilly kept pointing to the words in the songbook, but the excitement all around them drew their attention away.

Lettie could not get over seeing people act this way in church, and she wondered why she had goosebumps all over her when it was not cold. She was surprised at seeing how young the people were on the platform: both the young man in a suit and tie that called people to do things like lead songs or sing a special, and the people who sang and collected the offering were teenagers.

When the special singer came to the front, Lettie whispered, "He's in my history class!"

Debbie was wide-eyed throughout the whole thing, blatantly staring at the activities around her.

Eventually, people were seated and the preaching began. Another young man came to the podium, dressed in a tan suit with matching shoes. *Wow*, thought Debbie, *he must have more than one good pair of shoes, like Tilly.* She looked down at the dress and shoes she had borrowed from Tilly and was glad she had not worn her own shabby clothes. Then his words caught her attention as he read from the Bible.

"Seek ye first the kingdom of God and His righteousness and all these things will be added unto you." (Mt. 6:33) He went on to preach how His Kingdom and His righteousness go together. There were other scriptures, but that first one stuck in her mind. When the preacher talked about repentance and getting "right" with God, being filled with the Holy Ghost and his "righteousness," Debbie could not resist Tilly's invitation to pray for this experience. The three girls went to the front where others were praying.

Tilly and other church people prayed with Debbie and Lettie. The two girls were next to each other, but each had a different type of experience. Lettie wanted what the preacher and her friend had told her about, but in her mind, she kept thinking, *This is way too loud to be church. Can this be right?* She could feel something but held back, worried what her parents would think if she came home talking in tongues.

Debbie, on the other hand, was so desperate for change in her life that she prayed unreservedly, with tears and snot streaming down her face, following the instructions of a lady praying near her who said to raise her hands and talk to God.

"Help me, Jesus!"

"That's right, He's right here. He's listening. Tell him what you want."

"I need you, Jesus!"

There was a commotion near the front door, but Debbie was not paying attention to anything outside of this new and awesome experience. She felt something indescribably wonderful, like a river flowing through her and taking all the fear and pain of her life and leaving only joy and peace until the rough hand of her father grabbed her shoulder.

Immediately elders in the church laid their hands on Debbie's dad, not to hurt him, but they prayed earnestly in Jesus' name and Mr. Griffin fell to the floor. Prayer continued and God had more surprises in store.

Things didn't settle down for some time. Mr. Griffin talked in tongues for a long time, along with his daughter. As the baptismal pool was filled with water, Mr. Zygmunt called the Griffin home, then went to pick them up. Mrs. Griffin would not believe until she saw with her own eyes that her husband was going to get baptized and her daughter too!

Seeing was believing and tears of joy soon replaced her doubt. The whole church rejoiced loudly and were heard far and wide. It was getting late by now and the police came to quiet down the "wild party" reported by the neighbors.

As Mr. Griffin was leaving with his family, he turned to Tilly's father, "Mr. Zygmunt, you've raised quite a daughter there. I'm proud she and my girl are friends."

"Thanks, brother, and call me Zygi. Everybody does. God has sure done miracles in you and your family tonight!"

Tears began to gather in Mr. Griffin's eyes, "I wish my momma was alive to hear that her boy prayed back through."

"Prayed back through?" Zygi asked in astonishment as the family looked on with their jaws on the floor.

With a sheepish look, Debbie's dad gave half a grin and said, "Yeah, I never did tell my family about the church I grew up in." Tears began to flow again as he continued, "Looks like God is finally answering Mama's prayers."

The girls looked at each other, "and ours too," they said to each other.

There were hugs all around as the family turned to go. "Good night, brother Zygi, see you Sunday." Then he turned to his family, "Looks like you all got yourselves a new daddy tonight!"

❧

"Can you imagine how different that story could have been if Tilly had let her shyness keep her from helping Debbie?"

"I don't want to imagine it. I just want to thank you for all you have done!" She wrapped her arms around Jesus and said, "God, you are so good! I'm learning that everyone has more to offer than they realize."

EIGHT

Gigi
Mountain View, CA 1954-1975

"Are you ready?"

"Ready," Zella replied, looking up at Jesus. "What's this mission?"

"This is going to be a bit different."

A quizzical look on her face, Zella asked, "Different how?"

"Well, this is going to take a while. So far the missions you've helped me with were pretty short. But Gigi has a struggle with his temper, and there's no quick fix for that. It's going to take time."

"Then let's get started," Zella said as she jumped up and took his hand. She was now taller than his shoulder. A smile spread across her face, "I'm ready."

༼ༀ༽

Soon they were watching a church service in a tiny storefront building. A pretty woman with her hair piled up on her head sat in the front and played an accordion. An older man played the guitar, while a young woman shook a tambourine, her long hair flowing down her back. Front and center, behind the podium, a tall, thin man led songs for the congregation while his wife, Madlyn, sat near the front with their two children, a baby and a toddler.

Near the back, Zella recognized Elly and Gabe Pajaro with little Gigi, now three- and-a-half years old. The young boy was putting his ear to his momma's rounded tummy to listen for his little brother. He was sure it was going to be a boy. As Zella watched, a typical scene unfolded.

Tilly noticed that her mother was busy with her little sister, so she slipped to the floor and looked under the folding chairs. She could see Gigi's feet four rows back. In the blink of an eye, Tilly had crawled under the chairs and pulled on Gigi's pant leg, encouraging him to join her on the floor. Unfortunately, she accidently pinched his leg and made him howl. Instantly, Gigi whipped around and began to pummel Tilly. This unfortunate greeting produced screams from her as well. Their parents scooped them up and exited to the bathrooms.

ൔ

With Jesus at her side, Zella saw the fluttering of pages as time passed. A few years later, they are observing Gigi on the playground at school.

The shortest in his class, he is now in the fourth grade and waiting for his turn at tetherball. As a sore loser left the circle, he brushed past Gigi, pushing him out of his way. Instantly, Gigi was ready to fight. With his arms swinging, he went after the offender. Soon a teacher's whistle blew and the boys were taken to the principal's office. The black eye and bloody nose did nothing to assuage Gigi's anger.

Pages flutter again and Gigi, now in junior high, wanted to go to the school dance, but his parents did not believe in social dancing.

Why can't I go?" he screamed at his parents while pacing and gesturing wildly with his arms. "Everybody I know is going! I'll be the only one left out!"

"The answer is no. And if you continue to scream, you'll be grounded for a week as well. Now go to your room until you calm down."

"Aarrrgggh! This doesn't make any sense!" He wheeled around, stormed down the hall to his room, and slammed the door. His dad calmly walked into the room and commanded, "Now you can come out here and try closing this door properly." It took three tries, but eventually he got it right.

Jesus gave Zella that look that meant "Are you ready?"

She nodded in return, giving him a hug before he disappeared.

❦

"This is a tough one," she said to herself. She tapped her chin as she thought about what to do. Looking from parents to children she sighed, and got to work. "I see what you mean about this taking some time," she said.

Her first stop was Gigi's Sunday school teacher, Sister Louiza. She found her in prayer, seeking inspiration from God about her Sunday school class. The memory verse was Proverbs 25:28, "He that hath no rule over his own spirit is like a city that is broken down, and without walls." Sister Louiza asked God how she could make this come alive for her class in a way that would really help them. Gigi came to mind first, but this wise saint knew that self-control is a fruit of the Spirit that everyone needed.

Zella placed an idea into the teacher's mind and they both smiled.

Back at the little store front, Zella hovered over the classroom used for children's church. Sunday school in the small congregation consisted of six children, ranging in age from six to fourteen.

Timothy, Sister Louiza's son and the oldest in the class, came in early with his mom to help set things up. He was curious about the box his mother brought, and she told him how to play along.

They joined the congregation in time for prayer before service. Brother Zygi started service with a few congregational songs and then dismissed the children for Sunday school. They filed out to a little side room. Six chairs were crowded into the space that doubled as a storage area. After having the children read the memory verse, she announced a special visitor. "In just a minute, Sister Notlouiza will be visiting us. Excuse me," she turned her back to the children for a moment, putting on an old greasy apron and a messy wig containing a couple of dangling curlers. She inserted something into her mouth and turned back to the children.

Using a strange voice and accent, she greeted the class. "Howdy y'all!" She smiled, revealing several blacked-out teeth. The children gaped and giggled. Her expression turned fierce, "Whatcha all looking at? Don't you got any manners?" Their eyes got big as they wondered what they were supposed to do.

Brother Timothy went into action and greeted the visitor, "Glad to have you in Sunday school, um, Sister Notlouiza," he said trying not to snigger but failed.

"Why, thank you kindly," she answered, with a tilt of

her head, "glad to be here." She looked around the room, "'Course, anyplace is better than being home with that lazy good for nothing husband of mine. He got me so mad this morning I just let go and belted him a good one."

"Why did you do that?" Timothy asked, and the others chorused, "Yea, what for?"

"I'll just tell you why," she lifted her chin as she continued; "He took my pillow, that's why."

Puzzled faces looked up at Sister Notlouiza, "Wow, you hit him for taking your pillow? Couldn't you just ask for it back?" Timothy asked.

"Well, turns out it was his after all, but it's the principle of the thing. And he made me late for church. I didn't even have time to do my hair." She patted her hair and gasped in mock surprise when she found a curler. She took it out of her hair, made a fist, and declared, "I can't believe he didn't tell me I had curlers in my hair! I'm going to get him for this!" She turned around from the small group, took off her disguise, and said, "Goodbye, Sister Notlouiza."

Turning back around, Sister Louiza said, "Now, what do you all think about that? Who can tell me how our memory verse applies to Sister Notlouiza?" The discussion started out slow, but each one began to warm to the topic and easily listed many problems Sister Notlouiza had that stemmed from the lack of self-control: Sister Notlouiza looked unkempt and got mad at others for things that were her own fault. Class continued with a patience-evoking gluing craft and concluded with a snack. Later that afternoon Zella had another lesson for them once they were all home.

Gigi had three brothers and a sister. The rowdy bunch

came home hungry after being in church all morning. Mama was securing Ralphy and Milly into high chairs while Gigi put out mayonnaise, bread, and bologna. He pulled out the cutting board, got a large knife, and slapped together a sandwich, leaving the fixings on the counter and the cutting board sticking out from the cabinets.

Franky and Jonny raced in a moment later and the two of them dove for the knife. Franky, the older of the two, grabbed it and Jonny grabbed his wrist.

Mom saw the commotion and ordered, "Put down that knife! No wrestling in the kitchen! You boys know better than that!" That settled, she went to put away her purse and coat before preparing lunch for the little ones.

"I'm hungry, how come you get to go first?"

"I got here first, half pint."

"Not fair!" Jonny stomped and pouted while Franky made his sandwich in an exaggerated slow motion.

"Arrrggh!" Jonny grunted and stomped again showing his frustration.

Gigi had now finished his sandwich and headed back for a second. Jonny tried to head him off as Franky cut his sandwich. The scuffle began as Franky put the knife down. The yelling and pushing suddenly stopped as Gigi was pushed against the cutting board and the long knife shot forward as the cutting board slid in. They looked at the sharp point of the knife, so close to Gigi's side that it cut into his shirt. The three just stared for a moment, realizing that a fraction of an inch could have made a terrible difference. The crisis was avoid for this time.

Later that week, Gigi wanted to go out with some friends.

"Shane and Kurt are too old for you to hang around with, Gigi. We told you that before."

"But, we're buddies—they asked me to go!"

"They are in high school and drive their own cars. Even if they were younger, they are not the type of friends you need to hang around with."

"But Mom…"

"The answer is no."

A honk sounded from the front of the house. "Mom, they're here to pick me up!"

"You tell them you can't go."

"Arrrrggh!"

"Or do I need to walk out there with you?"

"I'll do it!"

Gigi stormed out of the house and down the driveway to their car, "Sorry guys, I can't go."

"Can't go!" Kurt whined. "What's wrong? Did your mommy say no?" he mocked and laughed. Then his voice changed as he asked, "Hey, we're gonna have some real fun. Just jump in the car, she can't stop you."

Zella drew Gigi's attention to the bat in the back seat that he hadn't noticed.

He asked, "You gonna play baseball?"

Kurt and Shane burst out laughing, "We're gonna play a way you never saw before. Come on, we'll show you. Jump in."

Just then his mom came out the front door, "Gigi, I need you in the house."

"You coming or ain't you?" Kurt asked.

"Gigi," Mrs. Pajaro called again, louder.

"Aw, let him go to his mommy," they taunted. "Guess

he's just a baby," Kurt jeered as the car screeched away.

Gigi kicked the fence and batted at the tree on his way toward the house. He slammed the front door and stomped to his room yelling, "I'm not a baby!" as he slammed that door too.

About a half hour later, Mr. Pajaro announced he was taking his sons to get their hair cut. On the way to the barber, the traffic slowed as they passed an ambulance at the side of the road. The medics were loading a bloody mess of a person into the ambulance. Quickly, Gigi put his hand over Ralphy's face to shield him from the awful sight. As he glanced back, he saw a baseball bat on the ground nearby. Further down the street Gigi spotted Shane's Mustang next to a police car. Shane and Kurt were both being handcuffed. Gigi felt sick to his stomach.

"Hey, isn't that Shane's car?" Franky asked.

"I'm sorry you boys had to see this," their dad said. "But maybe it's for the best. Now you know why you're not allowed to run with them."

Gigi was quiet the rest of the evening and didn't have much of an appetite.

Mr. Pajaro noticed his son's melancholy mood and tried to cheer him up. "Hey, Gigi, are you ready for Youth Convention next month? I think most of the church is going."

"I have what I need," he answered, gloomily.

"Your suit still fits you all right?"

His interest increased, "I think so, why?"

"Why don't you try it on and have your mother check it." Gigi knew what that could mean and got up quickly. "We don't want you splitting your seams at church." He punched Gigi's shoulder as he went to get his suit.

Mom could tell at a glance that Gigi had grown out of his suit, "This one's Franky's now. We'll have to go shopping."

"Can we go now?"

Mrs. Pajaro smiled and nodded at her one son who loved to go shopping.

ᴄᴙ

Wearing his new suit and sitting on the front row the first night of the youth conference, Gigi heard a message that made an indelible mark on his life. Brother Jones preached a sermon entitled, "Amnon Had a Friend," telling how Amnon took the bad advice of his friend and how it eventually cost him his life. Gigi was the first to the altar to pray that night. Tears and tongues flowed easily as he felt the awesome presence of God.

The weekend after youth conference was his cousin's birthday party. It was a barbeque in the backyard of their Willow Glenn home. The hamburgers had just been served when there was a popping sound and something whizzed by his ear. There were more pops and Gigi noticed a gun barrel over the top of the fence.

Everyone else hit the dirt, but Gigi took off after the culprits. His senses were on overdrive as he tiptoed through the parked vehicles. As he passed a truck, he caught a movement by his side. Immediately his fist went after the shadow. Unfortunately, it was his own shadow on the side window of a truck. Glass shattered and blood dripped from his hand and wrist. The crazy kids at the fence heard the crash, dropped their BB gun, and ran. Gigi came back to the party leaving a trail of blood.

At school the next day Tilly came up to Gigi at lunch. Her cheeks colored as she spoke. "How's your hand, Gig?"

"It's okay. I just feel so stupid."

"Well, I think you were brave. If it weren't for you, those kids might have really hurt someone."

Feeling a few inches taller, Gigi puffed out his chest and saluted, "Just doing my job," he smiled. They laughed together and the bell rang. "See you later," they both said. As he walked away he mused, *I've known that funny faced girl all my life*, and shook his head. *When did she get to be so cute?*

❧

The Pajaro family prayed together each morning and evening. Gigi began to notice a difference in his day when he made time to pray with them before school. These days he felt God giving him strength to control his anger. But some days, no matter how Zella pushed him, he would be rushed and not do much praying. Those days he would inevitably get into a fist fight. When that happened, Tilly would have nothing to do with him.

Gigi just couldn't see it was the prayer that had gotten him through. He just knew some days were good and others were out of control. He wondered if he could ever get off this roller coaster.

One Sunday during Gigi's senior year, there was an announcement at church about a building program. On the way home Gigi asked, "You think I can help, Dad?"

"We're all going to do our part, son."

Everyone was excited and talking at once. Soon the whole church was getting into a new routine; people came to the church site after work and on weekends. Women made food and brought it for the workers.

Gigi went every chance he had and worked untiringly right alongside the men in the church. During this time Gigi noticed something was changing about himself. He hadn't been in one fist fight since he began work on the church. There was something satisfying about working with his hands. It not only calmed him, but it gave him time to think and listen to the voice of God.

During this time, Tilly always had a smile for him and he was seeing her more often. After two months of no fist fights, Tilly agreed to be his girlfriend.

Gigi helped with all types of work through the construction, but when he began tiling, he found it was his favorite job. His parents had noticed the difference in him too, so that when he approached them about looking into an apprenticeship, they were happy to see what could be done. They found a program that combined on the job training with classroom time and paid for a portion of work toward the end.

ↂ

Mrs. Pajaro was almost done making dinner when she got a phone call. It was Gabe's boss at Juicy Fruit. "I'm sorry, Mrs. Pajaro, but I think Gabe had a heart attack. The ambulance came, but it was too late."

Stunned, Mrs. Pajaro looked over at dinner on the stove

thinking, *He's never going to be home for dinner*. Then the room became fuzzy and her thoughts froze. The sound of Gabe's boss droned in her ear.

"Are you there, Mrs. Pajaro? I'm so sorry, I know this is a shock, I'm shocked myself. Is there anything I can do?"

Pulling herself together, she asked, "Where's Gabe? Shall I go to the hospital?"

"Yea, that's right. That would be the place."

She hung up the phone, feeling strangely unreal. Her neatly ordered world had crumbled around her, and there was nowhere to turn but God.

The funeral was planned and crowds of relatives and friends came to offer sympathy and food.

Then it was over and all the relatives and friends had gone.

After a couple of days of crying and praying, Mrs. Pajaro gathered all the children.

"We're all going to have to pull together," she said, trying not to cry. "With your father…" she paused, struggling with the word, "gone, there will have be a lot of changes. I'm so sorry."

She felt strength from the prayer of the saints of the church. Taking a deep breath, she continued, "I'll get a job, and I need all of you to help too."

She looked up at her oldest son and felt her stomach knot. She had to tell him. "Gigi, we're going to need your help. I know you were looking forward to the apprenticeship, but, there's just no money for that anymore. I'm sorry. You're old enough to get a job, and, well, that's what we need you to do.

Gigi's mind flashed to driving in the car with his dad.

He could hear his voice and felt a mantle pass onto his shoulders. Then he spoke the words, "We'll all do our part, Mom."

She turned to her second oldest and saw a younger version of her husband. She rubbed her clammy hands on her skirt and continued, "Franky, you're old enough to get a work permit and find something part time while you finish high school."

"Sure, Mom, I can do that," came his hollow reply. It all felt like a bad dream.

Jonny, her tenderhearted thirteen year old, came next, "Jonny, what do you think about maybe cutting lawns or doing a paper route?"

A bewildered, "Yeah," escaped his lips as he looked around.

Elly wanted to help her child and began, "Your father always said," but her voice broke and the rest came out in gasps, "you do a great job on the yard." Bringing her hand to her face, she closed her eyes and tried to breathe normally but failed. Gasps and hiccups brought the family closer around to comfort her. She had so wanted to be strong for their sakes. *God help me*, she prayed.

"I can help too," Ralphy offered, thinking of another fourth grader with a paper route.

"Good, Ralphy, thanks." She dried her eyes and turned to her one and only girl. "Milly, you're getting so big. I think you'll be a big help around the house now that I will be working."

Milly nodded, "I know how to cook rice now, Momma, so I can help with dinner too."

"I think you're part Chinese," she teased as she tickled

Milly under the chin, causing the girl to squirm and giggle.

After giving her a hug, Elly took another deep breath to prepare for the worst news yet. Thank God it was the last bombshell. If this kept up, she would hyperventilate.

"One more thing." Everyone looked up at her expectantly. "We can't afford to live in this house. We'll have to move." They were frozen in time, shocked into silence. "I hate to spring this on you so soon, but I think it's better for you to know. Aunt Mary and Uncle Ralph have a vacancy in the apartments they own just two blocks away so everyone can stay in the same school."

Jonny wrinkled his nose, "An apartment? Won't it be kind of small?"

"Well, yes." She had to be honest. "It's a two bedroom, so…"

"Two bedrooms?" They all shouted in astonishment. Their current home had four.

"Yes. We'll work it out." She stretched out her hands to them, "Let's all pray together. We need God to help us in so many ways right now." They joined hands and prayed.

Gigi saw his dreams crumbling around him. It was hard for him to pray. His anger rose with each unanswered question. *Why do we have to move? Why can't we try to make it here? Why did my dad have to die? Why, God, why?*

High school graduation was in two weeks—big deal. A few days ago it would have been a happy occasion. A few days ago he had plans. After graduation he wanted to take his apprenticeship, get a job, and ask Tilly to marry him.

Now, with Dad gone, everything had changed. He still could not believe his father had died. Gigi thought of his father's strength. He replayed scenes in his mind of times

106

he had spent with his father; many times the two of them worked on a car, and when his dad had told him, "You have to know how to take apart an engine and put it back together before I'll let you get a car." He had done it—Dad had taught him how.

A tear made a glistening track down his cheek, and he wiped it with the back of his hand. He was walking around the backyard of their home, saying good bye. They were almost all packed up. Soon they would start moving to that little apartment. The thought of it made him sick.

They had all grown up in this house. He looked over at the lemon tree he had helped plant. Under it was the grave of Duchess, his first dog. *Oh, God, help me*, he wiped more tears from his face, *I hate this! My dad is gone! My past and my future are both gone! God, what do you want from me?* He punched at the wall of the house and hurt his hand.

As he shook his hand, he faintly heard a small voice, "Just trust me," as a heavenly peace settled around him. He looked around in wonder and then slowly walked back inside.

His struggle continued, even at church. Memories of his father produced an instant knot in his throat, and when it was time to pray, he stood stubbornly in his place. Zella gave Brother Brooks a nudge and he came to help Gigi pray. As he stood there, rigid and angry, he felt the elder's hand upon his shoulder and with it came the peace and love of God. The tears began to flow, and he was reminded that God really did love him.

Someone was singing, "We'll Understand It Better By and By." Others came to pray with him and added to the presence of God. Words of encouragement mingled together as his tough exterior melted away, and he prayed through to a new language again. As the Spirit lifted, he knew two things: God loved him and he wanted to have a touch from God like this more often.

Zella tried to get him out of bed to pray the next morning. She tried air in the water pipes that made a loud screeching sound when his mom turned on the shower. Everyone woke up. Gigi just pulled his pillow over his head and felt aggravated.

When he did finally get up, she tripped him with the tennis shoes he had left out the night before. This was meant to get him on his knees but just made him angry. She would have to change her tactics.

Zella tapped her chin, thinking. She knew he was in for a rough day, and that prayer would help him through. While he was in the shower she reminded him of the great blessing God gave him the night before. "You need to thank Him," she whispered, to no avail.

Sure enough, everything went wrong that day: he had a pop quiz in math, he'd forgotten the final project in another class, his lunch bag ripped and everything fell out— even seeing Tilly could not lighten his mood.

By the afternoon his blessing of the night before was a vague memory. Just when he thought it couldn't get worse, it did. Grabbing the mail as he arrived home after school, he noticed an envelope with his name on it. There it was— Luigi Pajaro—on an official looking envelope from the US government. He knew what it was: A draft notice.

Certain that he would be sent to Vietnam, he decided to take his chances and talk to Tilly. The next service was Wednesday night Bible study. As soon as church was over, he took her hand and led her outside.

"I have to tell you something." Before she could answer, he turned to her and continued, "I'm drafted, Tilly." The words rushed out, "I know I'll be going to Vietnam." Then, going down on one knee, he took her other hand, and looking into her eyes asked, "Tilly, please wait for me. I want to marry you when I get back." Tilly begun to cry as he asked, "Will you marry me?"

"Oh, Gigi!" she said through tears. When he stood she wrapped her arms around him, "Of course I will marry you! I've loved you all my life!"

Days passed in a blur of activity: Gigi's family moved to the apartment, they cleaned out the old house, he graduated and then reported for his army physical. After passing with flying colors, Gigi had a short time before he was to be shipped out to boot camp for basic training. The day before he was due to leave, he and Tilly talked over wedding plans.

"So what kind of wedding do you want?"

"The kind that makes me your wife." Tilly smiled up at Gigi as they sat together on the porch swing sharing a bowl of fresh strawberries.

Tilly's mom came out of the house as if on cue. "You two set a date yet?" She set down two lemonades on the table and looked expectantly at the young couple.

"We still have to figure it out." Tilly gave her mom a tight little smile. Why did her mom get on her nerves so much lately?

Mrs. Zygmunt was a bit edgy as well. She answered with a terse, "Fine," as she turned to go. She tried to soften it with, "I hope you'll let us know as soon as you decide," but it sounded huffy.

"Of course we will, Mom." Her mother disappeared into the house and Tilly sighed with relief. Looking at her fiancé she asked, "What do you want to do, Gigi?"

"I have a job now with the army. I wish we were already married and on our honeymoon." They both gave a nervous laugh. "Problem is we would have nowhere to live until after I go to boot camp."

Tilly placed her hand on his. "How about you just let me know when you will be on leave, and we can have a simple ceremony when you get here?"

"Don't you want to have a big wedding?"

"My parents want me to have a big wedding. I think it's the wedding they never had. You know, living through your children and all that."

"What about you?"

"I told you, I just want to be your wife," she smiled. "A marriage license and Pastor Kitchell is all we need. The rest is optional."

"You know our families would be ticked off if they were not there." Tilly sighed and nodded. "How about if we get the license now, and when I come home on leave we can do like old Brother I.H. Terry and set it up with Pastor Kitchell to have a ceremony at the end of Sunday morning service."

"But you leave tomorrow."

Gigi looked confused, "Yeah?"

"It takes three days for the blood test."

"Stupid blood test." Gigi kicked at the table leg and spilt some of the lemonade.

As Tilly mopped it up with a napkin, she went on, "We can still plan on getting the license and doing a simple ceremony while you're on leave. Surely there will be time to get a blood test…" Tilly cut short her thought as she looked back at Gigi. "What is it?"

Gigi took a deep breath and it seemed like forever before he spoke, "Tilly, what if I don't come back?" Strands of a popular song tickled his brain, *"Be the first one on your block to have your boy come home in a box."* But Tilly's response blocked it out for the moment.

"Oh, Gigi, I want to be your wife no matter what. And we are all going to stay prayed through, asking God to keep his hand on you and bring you back safe. You just remember that.

ભ

Gigi rolled into Fort Benning, Georgia, at about 3am, having not slept much on the bus ride there. Immediately the shouting began. "Get your *#* off the bus now! Move it!"

It was hurry up and wait. Scared and confused, Gigi rushed to get his bag and get in line.

This was the beginning of the most terrible and most wonderful experience of his life. There was no food and no sleep for the first grueling thirty-six hours. He was assigned a "battle buddy," a guy with an unpronounceable name and the whitest skin Gigi had ever seen. He and "Whitey" were to stick together at all times. In the barracks he was assigned to a "crib." It was a bunk bed. He took the bottom and Whitey took the top. Next to their crib was the tallest guy in the platoon.

He took one look at Gigi and said, "Hey, Shorty, where you from?"

Tall guy's battle buddy was on the lower bunk, a guy with a goofy grin on his pumpkin face.

At last it was time for chow. The line moved so slow it almost went backward. The tall guy complained, "Are we ever going to get some chow?"

Whitey imitated the man on "Kung Fu," squinting his eyes and changing his voice. He half whispered, "Ah, Grasshopper, you must learn patience."

Everyone laughed except Grasshopper's battle buddy. "Hey, what's so funny?" he wanted to know.

"Don't you ever listen to what's going on?" Grasshopper asked.

"Why should I? I got you to tell me what I need to know."

Grasshopper looked up to the ceiling, "Why me? Hundreds of guys here and I get animal head."

His buddy looked down sadly. Gigi gave him a playful punch, "That's right, Animal Head, stick with us and Grasshopper here. and everything will be all right."

The line finally moved. The four buddies ate together that day and went "to hell and back" together over the next fourteen weeks. They learned to march, care for and shoot a rifle (carried that seventeen pounds with them everywhere), and they took care of one another. They wrote letters home and shared news from home. Then it was time for graduation and new orders. The four buddies were shipped out in different directions, but they would never forget one another.

Gigi's contract was for Army infantry/airborne. He was excited about learning to fly, but he struggled with the thought of dropping bombs on people. Smacking around his little brother was one thing; blowing up a whole village was another. Zella put his Bible right in the middle of his bunk. He was surprised to see it there and, taking it as a sign from God, immediately began to read. She guided him to scriptures that gave him peace concerning the job that may lay ahead of him. He was reminded that God controlled all the nations and was responsible for who was in charge. He kept holding on to the Bible and prayed fervently, if quietly, in his bunk until the peace of God allowed him to sleep.

Gigi had a short leave before returning to Fort Benning Jump School. He contacted Tilly to set up their wedding. They did it Brother Terry's way, and all the family was there. Cake and punch were served in the fellowship hall before the two sped away in a borrowed car, fully decorated with tin cans and streamers, for a couple of nights near Monterey.

His leave was over way too soon. He had to say goodbye to Tilly for now but assured her that as soon as possible, they would be together again. Back at Fort Benning, three incredible weeks flew by, literally, as he learned to jump out of a plane.

Dear Tilly,

I am so excited, I was chosen for warrant Officer training and will be going to Fort Rucker, Alabama. This puts me on track for pilot training. God must have His hand in this. Some guys wait a long time for it. About Fort Rucker, I hear it is out in the middle of nowhere, but if you are there it will make it bearable. Once I get there I'll check everything out. I hope we can get a little apartment close by.

Good news! Before they ship me out from there, I'll have a two week leave. I fly on standby, so I'll call when I land at Moffett Field. Can't wait to see you,

Love you,

Gigi

The two of them stayed at the Zygmunt home—Gigi's family did not have any extra room in their tiny apartment. It was fun for him to get to know Tilly's little sisters. Anna was only a couple years younger than Tilly, but Zella was a surprise who came much later—she was only eight years old. When she heard her older sister would be moving to be with her army husband, she was thrilled. "Can I have your room?"

"Nice to know you'll miss me," teased Tilly.

Tilly was able to join him within a month. Gigi quickly moved through the training and advanced from helicopter mechanic to pilot training. Tilly kept a close eye on the news of Vietnam. They found a good church to attend while there, and the others in the church prayed with Tilly and Gigi about his orders. He was thrilled to be living his dream to fly a *Huey*. He barely remembered how he once had wanted to learn to lay tile for a living.

Toward the end of his yearlong training, he heard about the 1972 Paris Peace Talks and wondered if he would have to go to Vietnam. Maybe the war would end by the time his training was over. Gigi had mixed feelings; he had to admit it was an exciting thought to be in on the action in Vietnam, but he tried not to think about the possibility of not returning.

The peace talks did not go well, and Gigi finished his

training just in time to be part of President Nixon's "Operation Linebacker II," also known as the "Christmas Bombings."

Arriving in Vietnam in late October gave him time to run several missions before the big day. He had five other men in the *Huey* with him during each mission. Sometimes they dropped supplies to men in the field, other times they were part of an air attack, or flew the medic *Huey* to pick up the injured.

When December 18th arrived, he was assigned to a medic *Huey*. There were seven days of merciless bombings, mostly over Hanoi. They took off Christmas day and resumed bombing on the 26th. Unfortunately, this day off allowed the Vietcong time to regroup and be more prepared for the attack. It was during the last four days that two B-52 Bombers were shot down.

Gigi went into action. It seemed like he had super-human insight while maneuvering his *Huey* through SAMs (surface-to-air missiles), enemy fighter jets, and US bombs. Once he was sure he heard a voice yell, "Cut right!" just in time to dodge a SAM. And he couldn't explain how his hands and feet at times moved of their own accord, allowing him to see men on the ground that needed his help. As soon as the *Huey* was close to the ground, the men jumped out with stretchers, loaded the wounded, and slid them into place while enemy fire threatened on every side.

Back at the base, as the wounded were being unloaded, Gigi caught a glimpse of one of soldiers. The guy's skin was so white, could it be? He would have to check later; for now, it was back to the fray. By December 29th, after the last bomb was dropped and it was over, thirty US men had died and twenty were missing. He and the other *Hueys* couldn't get there fast enough to get them all.

That night Gigi had to check the men in the hospital to see if Whitey was there. He was tired to the bone, hungry, and spent, but this couldn't wait. He checked up and down the rows of cots. Finally, he came to one with that familiar white skin. Moving closer he could see those almost white eyebrows on the familiar face.

"Whitey," he said quietly to the sleeping soldier as he touched his arm. "Whitey, it's me, Shorty."

A lump came to his throat. "Whitey, can you hear me?"

Eyes fluttered, then a grimace and a cough. His eyes tried to focus, "Shorty? You did it, man. You brought me home." A pause and a half smile, then, "Thanks, man," before he closed his eyes again.

"Any time, bro."

The next day Gigi checked the MASH (Mobil Army Surgical Hospital) unit again first thing in the morning but couldn't find him. Asking a nurse, he learned that Whitey had died during the night. Thoughts of the letters home that were shared came back to him. Whitey had a mom, dad, and a sister waiting for him at home. Tears came to his eyes. The nurse said, "I'm sorry," as they both turned from each other.

Back home, peace demonstrations were plentiful, but the pile of rubble that used to be Hanoi brought the North Vietnamese back to negotiations. The Paris Peace Accords were signed on January 23, 1973, and the troops began to come home.

Gigi was so thankful that his time in Vietnam was short. He saw the mess that some of the other men were in after being there too long. Their nerves were frayed to such a point that no amount of R&R could help them. "Excitement" wasn't all it was cracked up to be. Oh, he loved flying his *Huey*, but the reality he saw on the battlefield and in the MASH unit was all too raw and real to desire any more such "excitement." Gigi said a silent prayer, *Thank you, Jesus, for keeping your hand on me and bringing me home in one piece".*

He thought he heard a voice answer, "Just doing my job."

❧

"And a fine job you did too."

Gigi's self-control is strong enough to get him through life now."

"It's amazing. We worked on him for twenty years just to develop this one thing." Zella shook her head. "It's a good thing you are patient, Lord."

"My children are my special treasure. You know I will do anything to help them get ready for heaven. I want them here with me forever."

Zella looked at the scars on his hands and knew he really would do anything for his children.

NINE

Zella's Discovery
San Jose, CA 1975-1982

"This mission is going to be different," Jesus said. He seemed somber as he took Zella's hand. "Are you ready?"

With a nod, the two of them were off on the now very familiar trip to planet earth. They came to a small home in a new neighborhood. Most of the yards were just dirt, although some had a lawn put in. Looking inside one home, they saw this scene unfold.

❧

"But we've been married for five years and we have no children! Can't we go to the doctor to find out why?" Tilly's tearstained face looked up at Gigi, pleading, "Please?"

His heart ached for his wife, but he was just a little afraid to find out that he was the problem. Tilly was such a perfect wife, he was sure it couldn't be her. "We can if that's what you want." Then he reached out to his wife, "Let's pray first." He held her in his arms and rocked her as they cried and prayed together.

In the doctor's office a few weeks later, both were seated across from the doctor waiting to hear the news.

"I'm sorry, Mrs. Pajaro, but I'm afraid you'll never be

able to have children." Then looking at Gigi he added, "We won't have to look further unless you request it."

Tilly was so stunned. It felt like the ground beneath her had collapsed and the world around her was strangely unreal. Her husband was saying something, but she may as well be underwater for all that she could hear.

Gigi looked back and forth between his wife and the doctor, then asked, "Tilly, are you all right?" When there was no response, he gently shook her shoulder, "Tilly, Tilly, can you hear me?"

The doctor stepped in, "She's received quite a shock. I'm sorry, let me get something for her."

He left the room and quickly returned to hold something under her nose. As she breathed in, she made a face and tried to move away from the smelling salts. The doctor kept them in place until Tilly began to blink and speak. "Stop!" She shook her head as if waking up and then hugged her husband and began to cry.

"She'll be okay now," the doctor assured Gigi.

Easy for him to say, he thought as he held his weeping wife.

"You two take as long as you like. I'll be in the other room if you need me." He left and softly closed the door.

It was a silent ride home, each of them in their own world of pain and lost hope. Gigi thought of his two younger brothers who already had children. Tilly's younger sister Anna had just found out she was expecting. Everyone was having children—everyone except them. As they pulled into the neighborhood, Gigi almost started to cry when he thought about how they had bought their home with the thought of having a big family. As they entered through the front door, the emptiness was profound. Unable to restrain themselves any longer, they collapsed upon each other and cried until they were spent.

"We could adopt, you know," Gigi suggested.

"But I want to have your child!" Tilly paused, "I guess I'm being selfish, but I love you so much. It wouldn't be the same if the baby didn't have your eyes and your smile and at least one of your dimples."

"You know what we need to do?" Tilly's eyes met his and together they said, "Pray." At first they held hands and prayed, but the desire and the pain was too deep to leave it at that. They had a good old-fashioned prayer meeting, praying until they touched the throne of God.

A couple of hours later they were refreshed and once again hopeful. "God has this all in His plan," Gigi said. "Don't you feel it?"

"Mm hmm," she answered. "God is still on His throne, and I still trust Him."

"You know what I think?"

"What?"

"I think we ought to keep trying to have a baby. Our God can do anything."

CR

Jesus turned to Zella, "We've got to skip forward a few years now—hold on!" They ascended out of the earth's atmosphere and then returned, this time to a hospital.

Zella turned a quizzical face to Jesus, "Why did we have to leave and come back?"

"Because you can't be in two places at once." Light

began to dawn on Zella's face. She looked up at him and he answered, "You were the answer to that prayer you just saw your parents have."

"I need to sit down and dance all at the same time." She shook her head in wonderment. "So, do I have a job here?"

"You sure do. There were some other prayers they had, and you are here to show them I heard and answered."

Jesus transferred the full scope of the plan in an instant. She smiled and said, "Thank you," as she looked into His eyes. He smiled back, "I love you," he said and vanished.

ɢʀ

Zella became her six-year-old self and sat on the bedside of her mother. Tilly was in pretty bad shape from the car accident that had taken Zella's life. "Momma," she whispered. Tilly stirred a little but did not open her eyes. Tilly tapped her arm, "Momma," louder this time, "It's me, Yella Rella." The old nickname came back to her, along with many other memories: her mother's scent, and how she would hold her and pray with her before she went to sleep.

Tilly opened her eyes a crack, saw Zella, and then her eyes opened wide. Tilly reached for her daughter, gathered her into her arms, "Oh, Zella, they told me you didn't make it. The car burst into flames and you couldn't get out. My baby, oh my baby," she breathed into her hair as she squeezed her tight.

Zella enjoyed the wonderful feeling of being held by her mother and wished she could stay there longer. Zella answered softly, "I just came back to tell you I'm okay. It's so beautiful where I live now, Mommy."

Am I going crazy, Tilly wondered? "But I can feel you. You are here; you are really here."

With a surprised look Zella answered, "Of course I'm really here. Jesus heard your prayers, Momma. Jesus sent me to tell you he loves you." Zella paused then added, "And I love you too, Momma."

"I don't understand…Zella don't leave me!" Tilly began to cry.

"Don't cry. Jesus takes good care of me. I'm growing too!" Then she disappeared but spoke again. "Just wait, you'll see."

Tilly was shaken, but after the visit she began to recover. Within a week she was allowed to go home. Gigi had been home for three days already, with his mother as his nurse. She'd brought her youngest two with her—Ralphy and Milly who were sixteen and fifteen respectively. Ralphy was driving now which made it possible for him to get himself and his sister to school and home from across town. His grin went from ear to ear when his mother handed him the keys. The feeling was not reciprocal.

After the drunken driver hit Gigi and Tilly head on, it was hard for Mrs. Pajaro to let her youngest son drive, but there was no other way she could think of for them to get to school without leaving Gigi alone, and she didn't want to do that. He was still too fragile. What if he fell and hurt himself again? No, she would have to let Ralphy take the car and trust Jesus to keep them safe.

Mrs. Pajaro found two old hospital beds at the second-hand store and had a friend pick them up and bring them to Gigi and Tilly's house. They had crank handles at the head and foot to raise and lower the bed as desired.

Both beds were in the large living room. Ralphy used one of the bedrooms, Mrs. Pajaro was with her daughter, Milly, in another one. The arrangement was working out. The stitches on Gigi's forehead were healing well and his ribs were improving too. The broken shoulder and shin bones would take longer to heal.

Zella visited Gigi in a dream early one morning. They frolicked in a meadow together and laughed until Zella heard someone calling her. "I've got to go now, Daddy. I'll see you later." She ran to the arms of Jesus and disappeared into a cloud. He woke up with a feeling of peace unlike anything he had ever felt.

Tilly, on the other hand, continued to comb glass out of her hair for weeks to come. She had a broken collar bone, a broken arm, and multiple bruises everywhere. She had tried to cover Zella with her own body; but in that nightmare moment, nothing would have helped. Her biggest injury was her broken heart. Now she battled depression. There were days when she just walked around like a zombie or went to the garden to grieve over her loss.

"I will never see her grow up. I wonder what she would have looked like."

A small memorial service was performed at the church once Tilly and Gigi could manage the trip. Just the family and church members were there. Everyone thought it would help Tilly and Gigi deal with their grief. They were wrong. Only God and time could help.

While Gigi's mom and siblings stayed with them, they would all meet in the living room for prayer before going to sleep for the night. Tilly wondered if she should tell them that she had seen Zella, but so far she could not bring herself to do it. Each one had a turn to mention prayer requests. When it came to Gigi he gave a crooked smile and said, "I have a testimony and a big thank you to God today." The family looked at him expectantly. "I saw Zella this morning."

A collective gasp, "What?"

"You too?"

Eyes swiveled from Gigi to Tilly and back.

"Let me explain. It was like a dream. The two of us played and laughed until she suddenly stopped and said she had to go." His voice cracked a little as he completed the story. "I watched her run into the arms of God. I can't explain how it made me feel." He paused and wiped a tear from his cheek. "I felt such a peace when I woke up. God is so awesome. I just want to thank Him for one more play time with Zella."

"Praise God!" echoed around the room and "God is so good!"

Then Mrs. Pajaro prompted Tilly, "Did you have something to tell us, Tilly?"

Shyly Tilly looked around as she tried to decide how to say this. "Yeah, I was afraid to say anything. I wasn't sure if I was unbalanced or something." She hesitated, looking around, "I saw Zella at the hospital. She came and sat on my bed. I got to hold her again." Then sobs began. "I miss her so much!" The family gathered around and prayed and cried with her until the peace of God enveloped them.

Tilly had times of peace, like the prayer meeting, but she would eventually lapse back into her grief. One day out in the garden, as Tilly prayed for deliverance from her grief,

Zella appeared to her again. Now she was the size of a twelve year old.

"Momma, why are you crying?"

Startled, Tilly looked up. Seeing Zella, she reached out to her, "Oh, my baby! Look how big you are! Is it really you?"

"Yes, of course it's me. Here, take my hand. See, I am still real. Don't cry, Momma. God still loves you. He still hears all your prayers."

Dumbfounded, her mouth opened but no words could be formed.

Zella put out her arms, "Can I have another hug, Mom?"

Tilly nodded, opened her arms, and gathered her dear girl into them. "Thank you, Jesus! Thank you, Jesus!" She repeated as she rocked back and forth with Zella in her arms.

"Thanks, Mom, you give the best hugs. I have to go now, but I'll see you again. I love you." She vanished, but not before Milly saw Tilly talking to a girl.

"Who was that and where did she go?"

Tilly jumped and turned around, "You saw her?"

"Well, yeah. Who is she? Does she live around here?"

"It was Zella." Tilly looked up at Milly. "It was like when I saw her in the hospital, only this time she was older."

"Yea, it did look like someone about twelve."

"I don't know how, but, she has already grown a few years." Milly came and sat by her sister-in-law and Tilly continued speaking. "I have to tell you something. This is so amazing." Tilly took Milly's hand. "God is so good!" A tear ran down her face, "You know, one of the things I sorrowed over losing Zella was that I would never get to see her grow up and look! God has allowed me to see her at an older age! I can hardly believe it!"

"God is awesome!" Milly agreed. "I wonder if I'll get to see her again."

"God only knows," Tilly shrugged.

"Oh, I almost forgot, your family called and are on their way over to see you. While they're here, your sister Zella and I wanted to work on a song for Sunday, if that's okay?"

"Sure," she answered, wondering that the usual sting of hearing Zella's name had lightened considerably. "Do you need any help with the music?"

"Your dad said he would play the piano for us."

"Hey, anybody home?" They heard Mr. Zygmunt calling from the house.

"Dad! We're out here."

When he joined them in the backyard, he took one look at his daughter and said, "Well, you look better than turkey dinner!" He smiled down at his oldest girl and gave her a big hug. "I could just gobble you up!" Straightening up he asked, "Say, I hear we're going to work on a new song. You want to go inside and listen? You've got a good ear so you can help us figure it out."

Tilly knew they didn't really need any help but was curious. "What new song are you talking about?"

"Your sister, Zella, wrote a song. Where's she at? Zella!" They heard piano music begin to play. "Oh, there she is." He smiled, "You up to it, sweetheart?"

"Sure, I'd like to hear it."

The melody was haunting, and it was still a work in

progress. They all listened as Zella picked out some notes. Then, her dad asked, "Why don't you sing it for us, Zella?"

"Okay. It's called, "Down by the Bridge." She picked up a paper and began to sing.

I'll meet you there on that eternal morning,
Light streaming down from the land above.
Loved ones there all are gathered
Down by the bridge

Down by the bridge, I'll take your hand
As you tell this world goodbye
We will walk into forever,
Where joy can never die,

Mistakes are all forgotten
As you leave this earthly place
Down by the bridge.
Down by the bridge
Da da da da da
In that land where we'll never die
Sweet flowers never fade
And we will never cry
We will change to be like Jesus
And see Him face to face
Down by the bridge.

Tilly had an eerie feeling that she could not place. When her sister finished singing, she asked her, "Where did you get that song?"

"That's the really cool part. On Saturday morning when

I was just waking up I was kind of half-asleep still lying in bed, and I could hear this song. It was so pretty and I didn't want to forget it, so I wrote down the words as soon as I could."

"It even said da da da da da?"

"Well, I couldn't remember all the words." They laughed together, and it felt good to laugh.

Once Gigi and Tilly could manage on their own, Elly and the kids moved back to their apartment and the house seemed so quiet. "I miss everybody," Tilly said.

"Me too," Gigi answered. "The place is too quiet. I think I'll put on some music." He looked through their albums and chose one to put on the phonograph.

"I'm going out to water the garden while dinner cooks. I always feel better in the garden," Tilly said.

As she went outside, she could hear someone singing. As she neared the garden, she could see a dark-haired young woman of about eighteen leaning over the herbs and singing, "Down by the bridge begins forever, in that land where we'll never die, sweet flowers never fade and we will never cry."

She turned. "Oh, hi Mom! I've got some parsley for you—could you use a bit more in your spaghetti sauce?"

"I think I could, Zella," she said, drinking in yet another miracle. "My, you've grown so fast!" She took in her dark-eyed girl with the dimpled cheek and held out her arms for a hug. Zella filled them and returned the hug, then backed up to look at her.

"You are looking well; I think it'll be a while before I see you again, but you'll recognize me, even if I'm grown, when you get to the bridge. I love you, Mom."

"I love you too, my miracle girl, but won't I see you before that?"

"I'm not sure, but one thing I do know—God has more miracles for you, Mom. You are going to be busy with my little brother and sister."

One hand went to her face and another to her tummy as she gasped, "Don't tease me, Zella."

"I wouldn't do that, Mom. Jesus really does hear your every prayer."

"Thanks, sweetie."

Zella pointed up and together they said, "Thank you, Jesus!"

"He is the miracle maker. And he is with you all the way."

Tilly took Zella's hand and pulled her toward the bench. "Sit with me for a minute, Zella." They sat and Tilly continued, "Tell me, how is it you have grown so fast?"

"Well, that's a long story, Mom. But it's all part of answered prayer." Tilly looked like she wanted to ask another question, but Zella continued, "I wish I could stay, Mom, but it's time for me to get back. I'll see you at the bridge!" Zella brushed her mother's check with a kiss, and disappeared.

ော

Back home in her special place, Zella stroked her favorite kitty, now grown to its full height. Jesus appeared next to her.

"I told you this mission was going to be different. You fulfilled it perfectly young lady."

Zella beamed at being called "young lady."

"It was wonderful to see my mom and have all the sweet memories return." She turned to Jesus and hugged him tight, "Thank you so much!"

"You got her thinking of good things again. The sorrow of losing you had blocked everything else out."

"You gave her hope. You reminded her she will see me again. And not just for a moment, but forever next time. Plus, you went over the top in giving her the promise of more children. I think I am just as excited as she is about having a brother and sister!"

TEN

Zygi
San Jose, CA 2014

"Hello young lady." They greeted each other with a hug and kiss on the cheek. "Ready for another mission?"

"Oh, yes! What can I do for you?"

"One of my servants could use a little cheering up, and a few more need waking up." Jesus turned to Zella. "What do you think?"

"I'm ready if you are." She smiled.

He reached out his hand, and Zella took it. "Let's go."

Soon they were hovering over San Jose Hospital. They zeroed in on a fourth floor private room.

❧

Old, gray, watery eyes looked out the hospital window at the weeping willows blowing in the evening breeze. He remembered them from when he brought his wife, Maddy, here years ago. His gnarly hand wiped at his unbidden tears as a sigh escaped his dry lips.

A pretty young nurse breezed into the room, checked his chart, and smiled up at him, "So you are the famous Mr. Zygi!"

With a low chuckle, he answered "Famous? Me? I don't

think so." He waved a hand to the empty room, "Just look at the crowd." His short laugh turned into a cough. Looking up he asked, "Say, where's Helen? Now, she's one good nurse."

With a sad shake of her head, Zella answered, "She has a bad case of the flu, but don't worry, I'll take good care of you." She fluffed up and arranged his pillows, bumping him with her elbow. Grabbing a large bottle of lotion, she squeezed a generous amount into her palm and dripped her way over to his feet, where she enthusiastically applied it as she massaged them.

"Eeoow! That's cold!"

As the lotion warmed, she moved to massage his leg and arm. He nodded and sighed contentedly at the massage on his left side but hardly felt a thing on his right. His recent stroke had left that half of his body useless. Finished with the massage, she leaned across the bed to gently replace his hand at his side. A book fell out of her pocket. "Oh," she exclaimed as she picked it up.

"What are you reading there?"

"The best book ever written!" she replied as she turned the book around. "The Bible!"

Zygi's eyes lit up, "Well, that's the best thing I've heard all day! Got any time to read some to me?" With a sad look on his face, he pleaded, "These old eyes don't work so well anymore, and I would love to hear some scripture."

Checking her watch, she looked around and answered, "Sure, there's nothing I'd like more." She sat on the visitor's chair next to the bed and opened the Bible. "Any special place you'd like to hear?"

"How about some Psalms?"

"Sure thing." Opening the Bible, her hands quickly found the scripture she wanted. "It is a good thing to give thanks unto the Lord, and to sing praises unto thy name, O most High: To shew forth thy lovingkindness in the morning, and thy faithfulness every night."

"Like music to my ears," he breathed through a wispy smile. "Please continue."

She read through the 92nd Psalm. Many passages spoke to the old man: "The righteous shall flourish like the palm tree; They shall still bring forth fruit in old age; the Lord is upright: he is my rock."

When she finished, he heaved a contented sigh, "Thank you so much. How did you know my favorite Psalm?"

"Must have been the Lord," she said as she smiled and pointed out the window. "It's a beautiful sunset, and God is making it especially for you."

"I used to tell my Sunday school class things like that," he smiled. His eyes looked away as the smile faded. "That was a long time ago. I doubt any of them remember me now."

"You'd be surprised, Mr. Zygi. Kindnesses and work done for the Lord are not forgotten. Now can I do anything else before I leave you to watch God painting the sky?"

"I'm fine," he answered. "Much better now. Thanks." After she left, he pondered her words. Did anyone remember him?

As Zella was coming out of a room down the hall, her supervisor met her with a steely glare. "You are only on room 307? You should be finished with this whole wing by now! What have you been doing?"

Zella gaped, looked at her watch, and tried to reply," It's only been thirty min—"

"Don't talk back to me! I'll write you up for insubordination if you forget your place again!" she hissed as she waggled a finger in Zella's face.

Zella watched the retreating figure of the head nurse pound down the hall. The Betty Boop design on her scrubs was stretched to the limit and was not a pretty sight. Shaking her head to clear the vision of Ms. Hillip, Zella hurried to the next room. Her hands were shaking from the encounter, and it was hard to think, but, a quick *Help me, Jesus*, brought peace and a clear mind.

She finished her shift without any problems, but she could not avoid another meeting with Ms. Hillip at the end of her shift. She had to pass on information for the night nurse, and that meant going to the nurses' station. Here, again, the woman could not say a kind word but berated her as if she had not done a good job.

ﾂ

That evening, Zella paid an unobserved visit to Pastor Billus during his usual time for prayer and Bible reading. She did her best to jog some memories. She watched as he told his wife he was going to the church to pray for a while. On the way there, he looked at the black starless sky and wondered how long it had been since he had watched a sunset.

Zella whispered in Zygi's voice, "God made that sunset just for you."

"Who used to say that?" he mused aloud. The face of his old Sunday school teacher, Brother Zygi, came to mind. He went into the church to pray, and Zella did not let up but continually brought thoughts of Brother Zygi to his mind. He remembered the lessons from that old Sunday school class, the safety pin everyone brought home one Sunday as a reminder to pray for missionaries, and of his teacher's favorite sayings: "God made you the way you are on purpose! You are part of his plan."

Zella continued to remind Pastor Billus how Bro. Zygi started the first Bible quizzing team in the church and was the coach for it. Fond memories continued to flow. This made the pastor began to wonder where old Brother Zygi could be these days. Sister Josephine came to mind, and Zella watched as the pastor dialed Zygi's granddaughter.

As the phone rang Zella watched his thoughts. He tried to remember where the family had gone: Tilly, his oldest girl, and her husband , Gigi, had retired and moved to some lake. Brother Zygi had two more daughters: Anna was with her husband who pastored up in Canada, and Zella had married and gone on the mission field somewhere in South America. Yup, Tilly's daughter Sister Josie would be his best chance of finding out anything. She still lived in California as far as he knew.

The following afternoon, as Zella entered the room, there was a visitor talking and laughing with Zygi. "Enjoy your visit, I'll check back with you later," she called as she exited the room, deciding that her schedule would work better if she went to his room last.

Zella continued from room to room, caring for each of her patients, and kept careful track of the time today. Whenever she returned to the hall, she could hear the muffled tones of talk and laughter.

As she left her last room, sounds of prayer could be

heard. She was just getting out the meds for room 312 and didn't realize Ms. Hillip was right there until she boomed in her ear.

"Nurse Zella!" This made her jump, spilling the handful of pills onto the floor. "You are the most inept nurse I have ever seen! How on earth did you ever get a job?"

"I'm sorry, Ms. Hillip," she said, just managing to stop herself from saying, *You scared me.* She quietly bent down to pick up the pills from the floor. Ms. Hillip raged on, again leaving Zella shaken and feeling worse than before. Once she had gone, Zella took a deep breath, looked upward and silently asked, *Why is she like that?*

"You really want to know?" Jesus questioned.

Zella wondered if she could help this wretched soul as well somehow. The Lord gave her a glimpse of Ms. Hillip's life, which brought Zella some understanding. "God help her," she prayed, "and show me if there is something I can do."

When she left her last patient, she saw a tall gentleman leaving Mr. Zygi's room and walking toward the elevator. Checking her watch, she grinned as she headed toward Mr. Zygi's room. A smile lingered on his face, which made him look years younger. Two flower arrangements were on the side table.

"You're looking quite well today, Mr. Zygy. I think that visit did you a world of good and look at these beautiful flowers!"

He shrugged, "They must be for the famous Mr. Zygi," he smiled and lapsed into coughing. When the cough subsided, he explained, "The bouquet is from my grand-daughter, and the arrangement is from Pastor Billus," he answered. The words tasted like candy to his lips. "He was in my Sunday school class years ago, a fine young man who pastors a church in Lompoc now."

The following day, there were two women in his room. Gray streaked hair was piled up on their heads attractively, and they both had on sweaters even though it was hot outside.

Leaving another room, Zella heard sounds of prayer floating in the air and could just make out, "In Jesus' name" before hearing their heels tap down the hall toward the elevator. Entering his room, she saw his happy face and two more flower arrangements as well as cards on the side table. She shrugged in question; he shrugged back. "The famous Mr. Zygi," they said together, enjoying the moment with a shared laugh.

They chatted as she checked his vital signs and applied lotion. "My granddaughter came and sang for me. I love to hear her sing. She sounds a lot like my sweet Maddy did."

"What a treat! You are so blessed, Mr. Zygi. God has given you a good life, hasn't he?"

"I can't argue with that; I've been counting my blessings all day. In fact, that was one of the songs I asked her to sing. That one, and 'March around the Throne One Time for Me.' You know it?"

"Indeed I do, Mr. Zygi. Was your daughter one of the ladies that just left?"

"No, they were in my first Sunday school class. Just the two of them—they were the whole class that first day. Maddy and I team taught, and the class quickly outgrew the little room we had." He mused for a moment before continuing. "They brought that vase there with the card.

Sweet ladies now, you'd never guess what they were like back then."

"Oh, really?"

"Yes, they started coming in the bus ministry when they were just little things, barely in school—hair never combed, clothes they had worn all week, no manners. But little by little, the families in the church would bring them home for the afternoon to play with their children. They received some hand-me-down clothes and started looking a lot better.

"Our children were grown and we had no hand-me-downs for them, so one Sunday we took these two shopping. I think we had more fun than they did!" He smiled at the memory. "My wife, Madlyn, started to fix their hair and found it was full of lice," he made a face, "so we made a quick trip to the drug store. Maddie spent hours cleaning out their hair." He paused and scratched his head, "Feel itchy just thinking about it."

His laugh morphed into a coughing spell, and he could barely get his breath. The pneumonia was getting worse. Zella glanced at the "Do Not Resuscitate" sign above his bed as stealthy hands rigged him up to a breathing treatment. She adjusted the drip in his I.V. to make him more comfortable. His breathing improved and he nodded off to sleep.

The week continued with visitors, cards, and flowers. By Friday the room looked like a florist shop. His granddaughter had found sitters for her three children and was with him on her third visit. The sun had just set, and the room began to dim. She could see he looked tired. Getting up to leave, she asked if he wanted the light on.

"No, thanks, but I would like us to pray before you go."

"Of course, Papa." She took his hand, and they prayed together as the light in the room intensified. They could feel a strong presence of God with them. Suddenly, he squeezed her hand. Lifting up his head and other arm, his radiant face looked heavenward.

"You've come!" he exclaimed in his last breath. Gently he laid back, a rapturous look still upon his face and the once useless arm lifted, coming to rest upon his breast.

Josie looked up and back to her grandfather as she quietly began to sing,

> March around the throne where all the angels
> used to trod,
> You'll be in the presence of a never failing God.
> Sing the songs of Zion, Shout the victory,
> And march around the throne one time for me."

Tears spilled down her face and splashed onto their hands. Her usually strong voice cracked as she finished the last line of the song. She wiped her face with the back of her hand and bent down to gently kiss his cheek. She breathed in his scent with a final hug. Straightening up, she touched his face, saying, "Meet you at the throne, Papa."

ଔ

> Good-byes below and reunions above,
> Tears flowing down here for someone you love.
> Rejoicing rings loud for he passed the test
> His crown showing he loved Jesus the best .

He trusted and served though the days were long
God's Spirit sufficed, flowing into song.
His hands to the plow, he didn't look back
Walking with Jesus, he held to the track.
Through good times or bad, hard times, and trial
He stayed true to Jesus every long mile.

Justin, Zygi's youngest grandson, finished the poem he had written for the funeral, and his sister Josie came to the podium.

"Papa asked me to sing this at his funeral." Willing herself not to cry, she began to sing. Her lovely voice rang out, "March Around the Throne One Time for Me." She invited those gathered to join her in singing, and something started to happen.

Justin began to march around the church. Others began filing out of their seats and into the aisle. Brother Zygi was known for beginning a victory march in the church. Now he was evidently doing it again. But this time, there was the feeling of a mantle falling on a new generation. Josie took the cordless mic and joined the others, her voice remaining clear and strong this time until she reached the back of the church where an audible sound of wind entered the room. The Spirit of God touched her in a dance and moved like a wave from back to front until the music ceased and there was not a soul untouched by the presence of God. It was a true celebration of a saint of God making it to the other side.

Above that merriment another group joined in the jubilation. Ageless feet danced on streets of gold. The reflection of the heavenly mirrored in the service below. Zygi, Maddy, Zella, and many more celebrated together in the eternal city.

No telling how long they were living it up. No one ever got tired or out of breath here.

The Lord turned to Zella, now fully grown, "Now, that's what I call getting cheered up!"

She answered, "No one can put things together like you can, Lord! Your ways are best, and I love you!"

"And I love you," he answered.

Epilogue

Light seemed to come from everywhere. Tilly looked around and could just see the approach of a bridge. She realized she was standing, which was something she hadn't done for some months now. Stepping closer, figures appeared. "Mom," she breathed. "Dad! Zella!" She ran to take them in her arms.

"Told you I'd meet you at the bridge, Mom," Zella held out her hand and Tilly took it. The group moved across the bridge and the light intensified.

"It's better than I ever imagined."

"You ain't seen nothing yet!" Zygi smiled.

She felt what she could only call boundless joy and peace as they stepped closer to the light.

At the other end, a figure waited with outstretched arms.

Tilly caught her breath, "Jesus!" she breathed, and couldn't help but run to him. He wrapped His arms around her in a timeless embrace.

As they parted, his gentle voice greeted her, "Welcome home, my child. Enter into the joys of the Lord." He motioned to an incredibly beautiful landscape surrounding them that made her garden back on earth look pathetic.

Her eyes adjusted to the brightness, and she saw Zella holding her hand out to her. "Ready for a tour, Mom?"

Tilly hesitated, hating to leave Jesus' side.

"I am with you wherever you go," he said.

Tilly looked up into that face she had so longed to see.

She would love to just gaze upon him, but with his prompting, she followed Zella.

Zella showed her mother the heavenly nursery where she lived when she first arrived, and Madlyn and Zygi took turns showing her their special places. Eventually, they all settled in for a visit by the Crystal River.

"It's a good thing I've got a new body, my old one could never have taken so much joy!"

Everyone laughed, then Zella said, "God is so, so, so much better than any words can say!"

"Yes, He is," her mom agreed. After a pause, she said, "Can I ask you something?"

"Sure, Mom."

"You were named after your Aunt Zella, but Momma told me she got the name from your Grandma Elly." Tilly shrugged shyly. "I always thought it would be great to meet the original Zella when I got here."

Zella smiled and waved. Tilly looked confused. She began to speak, but Zella spoke first, "Let me tell you a story." The story began with a small Elita. "God gave me the desire to grow up. I didn't realize that that desire was in answer to your prayer until later." She smiled at her mom then continued, "This desire led me to many adventures on earth. We called them missions. The first one was with Harvey and Birdie."

They appeared for the telling and Zella introduced them. Little Harvey and the rest of the family came to meet the new arrival as well.

"So Jesus sent Zella here to lead Mr. Williams' good mare off the road just in time for us to meet. That was a turning point in my life for sure," said Big Harvey."

"Isn't God good!" Zella smiled and everyone agreed.

Tilly smiled and said, "That's great, but I still don't get where Grandma Elly's friend came from."

Elly and Gabe came to greet them. "Did I hear my name?" Elly asked.

Tilly jumped up to greet her old neighbor and mother-in-law. After they hugged, Tilly continued, "Wow! This is so awesome! Can you really hear us talk wherever you are?"

"Well, we knew you had arrived and so we headed this way."

"So is it true that my mom got the name Zella from a story you told her?"

"Something like that, yes."

"Let me tell you about the next mission I had, Mom. Then I think you will understand. It started with a little girl who was feeling left out."

Elly's sister, Faith, joined in, "Of course we never meant to leave her out. You know how kids can be."

When the story was ended, Tilly looked back and forth in amazement. "But how?"

They answered, "God can do anything."

Tilly looked around, "Wow, and I thought I saw Jesus do some great miracles on earth. There are so many more that I didn't see!"

"That's right," came the voice that Tilly didn't recognize. "Jesus cares about everyone and everything—big things and little things."

"Do I know you?" Tilly asked.

"My name's Cissie, I'm Birdie's sister, but your daddy knows me as the lady who sat next to him on the bus ride home from King City."

Again Tilly looked confused.

Zella asked, "You remember your dad's testimony about how two old people picked him up when he was hitch-hiking?"

"Yea," she said looking around suspiciously. "Is there more to that story?"

"A little," Zella smiled. "Little Harvey and I were the ones in the car."

Tilly's eyes widened, astonishment clung to her face like frosting on a cake.

Cissie continued, "Well, we could hardly let you grow up without a daddy, now could we? God heard your momma's prayers and pulled on his heart. We just gave him a little nudge in the right direction."

Zygi, Tilly's dad, wrapped it all up, "So, strangely enough, I met my granddaughter before my daughter was born. How do you like that?"

"God sure does work in strange ways!" Tilly confirmed.

Zygi continued, "Thank God I listened to that still small voice to call my girlfriend." He paused for a moment, then added, "I wonder how many lives are changed by one fateful time of listening to the voice of God."

The group nodded, then Zygi did what he used to do very well, "I think it's time to thank Jesus once again. What do you say? Let's head over to his throne."

He started the old favorite, "March Around the Throne One Time for Me." They all followed, hands lifted, and voices strong.

About the Author

Anita Tosh lives in Sunnyvale, California, with her husband of over forty years, her children, grandchildren, and two miniature schnoodles.

She has attended the same apostolic church for more than thirty-five years, taught Sunday school for more than twenty years, and directed the church preschool for eighteen years.

An avid Bible teacher, she has also spoken to ladies groups and church gatherings and writes devotionals for Christian magazines.